C000062772

# FEEA

## A Tale of Old Glasgow

With Sketches and Drawings
By
David Faulds

ISBN : 978-1-291-64701-3

# Preface

The bulldozers crush and hide the past as they rumble, relentlessly, down
the road that leads to change. These metallic, latter day dinosaurs wreak
havoc on our fondest memories, while our links with the past are buried,
unceremoniously, in unmarked graves; there are no marble headstones for
these cherished loved ones.

Glass, concrete and steel are vulgarly erected on these 'hallowed grounds'
and the vision of what once was, is hidden behind the screen of 'change for
the sake of change'; the charlatan who hides behind the guise of progress.
But there, in the dark recesses, quietly waiting under the mighty monoliths
of this great city, there, whispering in the shadows, the ghosts of the past
are restless. For, although their truth is buried, its tendrils are slowly
reaching for the surface and, one day, just like flowers, their stories will
bloom in the sunlight.

David Faulds

# Prologue

The dark closes and back alleys were a sanctuary to the poor
wretches who lived on the streets of Glasgow at the beginning of the nineteenth
century.

Life in those far off days was a dire struggle to survive the rigors of disease and
starvation, especially for those, unfortunate enough, to be living on the streets.
There were many characters that wandered those filthy, vermin ridden streets
and alleys. They were like a band of wandering performers, or misfits who had
escaped from one of the freak-shows that, sadly, were a form of entertainment in
those days.

This is the sad and tragic story of one of those pitiful wretches.

He was a young boy, an urchin who danced on the streets for coins and went by
the name of Feea.

No one knows where Feea was actually born; only that he lived with his parents
in a dingy room at the bottom of lower Stockwell.

It was believed that they had moved there from the Western Highlands, just
before Feea's fourth birthday. Not much is known about them, only that,
although they were desperately poor, they were, none the less, honest, law
abiding citizens.

Feea was in his fourth year, when, tragedy struck.

His mother and father fell ill and died within months of each other.

Even at such a tender age, he was cast onto the streets to fend for himself and
survive as best he could. He was like a wandering, helpless babe amidst a pack
of baying wolves. He slept in the dark corners of filthy alleys or in doorways or
back-closes. He scavenged for food in the dungsteads at the back of the
crumbling tenements near Glasgow Cross. If it was a wet night he could be
found huddled under the straw in the corner of an old, rat-infested stable.

Even under these dire circumstances, he managed to smile and generate a warm, friendly aura that stayed with him throughout his life.

He had an, almost, angelic countenance and by the time he had reached his eleventh year, had the stature of an athlete.

Some say that he was simple-minded; possibly due to the circumstances that forced him onto the streets in the first place, who knows. We only know that he was well liked by the children who attended the Grammar School. Socially, they lived in a world that was totally alien to the world of Feea, yet these children seemed to understand and even admire him in their own, innocent way. He played all their games and was a real champion at most of them.

The boys understood the terrible life that their friend led and in their own way, tried to help by giving him a little of their food, or, on occasion, an old jacket or a pair of trousers. Whenever they showed such kindness, Feea would bow low and kiss their hands with an elegance more ascribed to one born into 'the nobility', rather than that of a street urchin.

So this is the main character in this amazing and, sometimes, harrowing account of life, or maybe I should say, existence, in Glasgow at the beginning of the nineteenth century.

This is Feea and this is the story of his incredible and tragic life.

# THE MISTS OF TIME

1880 A.D.

It was Hogmanay and there were only a few minutes to go before the church
bells would ring in the New Year.

The stillness of the night was disturbed by a lonely barn owl hooting somewhere
in the valley while a mist rolled in from the sea and made its way into the Clyde
estuary.  Slowly it drifted inland, obscuring the river and hiding the small boats
along its bank.

In a small holding on the hill, above the village of Port Glasgow,
Old Hamish MacCurdie put another log on the fire, causing a shower of sparks
to fly up the chimney.  The old man made his faltering way back to the table in
the centre of the room, where Jean, his wife, was giving the final touches to the
small spread that she had prepared for "The Bells".

Midnight arrived with the sound of church bells pealing in the village, followed
by the bells and foghorns on the Tall Ships at the Tail o' the Bank.  The
crescendo faded, only to be replaced by a rendering of "Old Lang Syne" coming
from a dozen or so houses in the village.

With shaking hands, old Hamish poured some sherry into two glasses and
handed one to his wife, he raised his;

"A guid New Year tae yae lass an' monae o' them."

The old woman raised her glass;

"An' the same tae yersel' Hamish."

They smiled; it was a smile of warmth and understanding.

They put their glasses down and gave each other a gentle hug.

The old woman went over and sat by the fire as Hamish crossed over to the
sideboard near the door.  He opened it and took out an old lacquered box, the
kind that old people keep their valued treasures in; a box of memories.

Gingerly, he placed it on top of the sideboard.  The effort made him light headed and he felt a sharp pain in his chest which caused him to gasp for air. He staggered sideways and grabbed the edge of the sideboard; stopping himself from falling over.

The old woman turned round.

"Are you aw richt, Hamish?" The urgent concern in his wife's voice made the old man lie.

"Aye, it wis jist a wee stagger, ah'm fine, lass, ah'm fine," he assured her, she wasn't convinced;

"Yae dinna look fine. Ah dinna think that yae should gang oot there the nicht."

"Och, hod yer wheesht wummin, yer fussin' aboot nuthin'," the old man said with a smile that hid the truth. The old woman smiled back and shook her head;

"Yer an awfy man," she whispered to herself.

The old man turned back to the box and lifted the lid; the pain in his chest had eased a little.


The box contained a dried rose, an old bible and something round that was wrapped in a black velvet cloth. This he took and put it in the pocket of a coat that was hanging on the back of the door.

He lifted the coat down, and with a bit of a struggle started to put it on.

The old woman got up, crossed over to him and helped him into it.

"If yer no' feelin' weel, could yae no' leave it this year?"

Hamish turned to face her;

"Och lass yae ken thit ah dae this jist efter "The Bells" every year, it's a wee tradition tae me an ah widnae want tae brak it noo. Oany wie ah'm feelin' fine."

The old woman picked up a scarf and put it round her husband's neck.

"Yae'd better wrap up weel, its gonnae be awfy caul' oot there the nicht. Dae yae no' want me tae come wae yae, jist this time?"

Old Hamish put his hands on his wife's shoulders and with a smile, looked her straight in the eye.

"Wull yae stope fussin' wummin, ah'm aw richt." He gently kissed her forehead. "Noo awa an' sit doon, a'll be back afore yae know it."

The old woman turned, and with a smile that was not entirely convincing, slowly went back to her chair.

Hamish put his hip flask in his pocket and wrapped his scarf around his neck. There was a click as he lifted the latch and opened the door, he turned and looked back at his wife, who was gazing into the fire. The old man smiled, a smile that was warmed by love and a touch of sadness, and then with a sigh, he went out into the night.

When the door closed, old Jean looked towards it as a melancholy feeling came over her; she went to call her husband's name but instead, turned and gazed at the flames dancing round the logs in the fire.

Hamish made his way round to the back of the house and with faltering steps, started to ascend the small hill that was his back garden. When he reached the top, he sat down, gasping for breath, on an old wooden bench that he had put there many years before. It was positioned to afford the best view of the River Clyde.

It was a clear crisp moonlit night with a hint of frost on the grass.

The sky was a myriad of stars shining down from their timeless constellations. The sound of singing drifted up from the village and mingled in the stillness of the night. The old man sat there, a lonely silhouette in the moonlight. The mist had filled the valley and was slowly creeping up the hill to where he was sitting. The pain in his chest had eased a little, only to be replaced by a dull pain in his arm that he put down to the cold air getting to his old bones. He gave his arm a brisk rub to get some warmth into it, and then he took the object that was wrapped in velvet from his pocket. He placed it on the bench at his side and unwrapped it. It was a smooth, almost spherical stone. Lovingly, he ran his fingers over it and then took his flask and opened it. He stood up and, taking the stone in his left hand, held it to his chest. Raising his flask in a toast, he looked up the mist-covered valley.

"Here's tae yer memory, Feea, a'll ne'er furget yae," he said with a heavy heart. He sighed, wiped a tear from the corner of his eye, and took a drink from the flask.

Just at that moment, the song, 'Killiecrankie' could be heard drifting up from the town.

The old man held the stone tighter; "Dae yae hear that, Feea? It wis aye yer favourite".

He sat down and as he listened to the song, he let his mind drift back through the mist of time, back to where it all started.

Back to Old Glasgow, all those years ago.

## ARRIVAL

It was early summer.

A young couple stood on the deck of a clipper as it sailed up the Clyde towards its berth at The Broomielaw in Glasgow.

Callum McConachie put his arm round his wife Mairi, and held their little boy close to his side as they stood in silence, looking at the city and the tall buildings that stood back from the river. This was a far cry from his home in the hills of Sutherland and the tranquillity of the highland glens

The three-year old child looked wide-eyed and in awe at the great metropolis that was Glasgow.Feearchur was an only child, his parents affectionately called him 'Feea'.

The wharf was a hive of activity as they disembarked from the old sailing ship with their scant belongings. Clouds of dust rose into the air as sacks of flour were piled up on the dockside, ready to be collected by the numerous carts that were lined up along the Broomielaw.

There was quite a din as the dockworkers shouted instructions to each other amidst the noise of crates and boxes that were being stacked along the quayside. The McConachies made their way into town in search of accommodation but all they could find was a damp, dingy room on the ground floor of an old dilapidated building in the Lower Stockwell, this squalid hovel would be their home.

Feea's father, who was not in the best of health, fell ill and died a few months after they arrived leaving his mother to provide for both of them. Near the end of the year she also fell ill and was laid up in bed, leaving Feea, who had just passed his fourth birthday, to fend for himself. For a four year old, this was no mean task, as Glasgow was not very friendly to waifs and strays; being made up of two classes; those who had and those who would never have. Unfortunately, Feea fell into the latter category and that's where he would remain.

The old town, on the most part, was filthy and crawling with vermin. On a hot day the stench was overpowering, as the streets and alleys were no more than open sewers. There were piles of rubbish and decomposing food everywhere. The poorest part of the town seemed to be sitting on a nest of rats that could be heard, squeaking their heads off throughout the night. On occasions, when they moved from one building to another, usually in the early hours of the morning, it was like a black, slimy, shimmering mass flowing between the crumbling tenements.

Poverty was rife in the city. Beggars and vagabonds roamed the streets; either singularly or in small groups as a means of protection, for there were many unscrupulous ruffians hanging about in the shadows, ready to pounce on an unsuspecting victim.

Then, there were the resurrectionists, (body-snatchers).

Glasgow had its own version of 'Burke and Hare'.

They crept about the back alleys in the early hours of the morning, looking out for some poor beggar who might have died in his sleep, or, when they were desperate; help one of them on their way.

They didn't only rob graves; a fresh corpse was worth more than one that was already buried and a lot easier to acquire. This despicable crime was rife in those dark days when the human body could be, unscrupulously bought and sold.

There were also honest, hard working folk who made a living by toiling at their weaving looms and being exploited by unscrupulous merchants.

The children of the poor were submitted to intolerable cruelty.

They were made to work under the most appalling conditions, whether it be in workhouses, coalmines or as labourers to chimneysweeps. Most of them were bonded to the job they were involved in and were vulnerable to the abuses that took place there, yet even they were 'better off' than the children of the streets; the urchins.

They, on the other hand, were looked upon as filth and scum, the 'dregs of society'.

This was the uncaring world in which Feea was to live and somehow, survive. He would be a lonely angel in a hell full of devils; for him, in his vulnerable innocence, there would be no hope of deliverance.

He would create a little world of his own, and there, in his loneliness, would find a simple form of happiness.

## OLD ANGUS

Wullie Balornock made his way down the Saltmarket. He checked to make sure that the padlocks were secure on the premises that were on his beat. Wullie was one of the two policemen who patrolled the area around the city centre. He was well liked and respected by the people who lived and worked there. He was in his early thirties, tall and slim with an air of authority in his gait.

It was a bitter, cold night, typical for the start of the New Year that was only a few hours old.

This year it was Wullie's turn to do the nightshift.

The revelry was spreading onto the streets as the 'first footers' wandered to their chosen destinations. They could be seen clutching the customary Ne'erday bottles and traditional pieces of coal, while doing, less than justice, to some old Scottish songs.

Some of the renderings were a veritable assault on the eardrums but they were full of happiness and merriment; a scarce commodities in those days.

Wullie reached the bottom of the Saltmarket and turned into the Broomielaw. He walked along the street until he came to the Customs Shed that stood next to the river. This was the place where bonded goods were stored before being shipped to far off destinations.

He rapped on the heavy wooden gate with his cudgel. There was no answer. He did it again, then called out; "Hullo!.. Angus are ye there?"

A sound of shuffling came from behind the gate, it got louder, until the glow from a lantern could be seen through the gap underneath.

"Wha is it? Wha's there?" Came a high-pitched voice at the other side, it was almost hoarse with a distinctive dialect that originated from the Kingdom of Fife.

"It's me Angus,..Wullie,..Wullie Balornock", the tall policeman answered.

There was the screeching sound of an iron bolt being drawn, then the gate opened, revealing an old man, bent over with age and holding a glowing lantern in his shaking hand.

"Och its yursel' Wullie, come awa in an' wa'rm yursel,' " the old man said; pushing the gate open a bit wider.

Angus was the night watchman. He was in his late seventies, an old soldier who had seen many a battle but he never spoke about them as it was too painful to remember the friends who had fallen in far off lands. Their memory was very dear to him and he kept it locked away in his heart.

Angus was a lonely old man who never married. He was a proud old warrior who wouldn't give up, until, through old age, he was forced to retire from the army. The army had been his life, his passion and his home. Proudly he had marched to the pipes and drums of his regiment as they entered the battlefield in some far off land. Now he stayed in a dingy old room in a rat-infested tenement at the bottom of the Stockwell, one of the poorest parts of the city; a forgotten warrior alone in a battlefield where the enemies were poverty and disease.

The well, after which the street was named, was still in daily use and young servant girls would be seen carrying pitchers or 'stoups' of water as they made their way back to the big swanky houses where they were employed. Those residences were known, locally, as 'The Big Hooses'.

Most of the girls came from the Western Highlands and could be seen dancing round the well and singing in their native Gaelic tongue.

They made a pretty picture in their clean, bright, colourful aprons and were a welcome relief from the filth and grime that surrounded them.

Angus bolted the gate and then he and Wullie made their way into a large shed. It was empty, except for a few casks at the far end and a glowing brazier in the centre.

Before they sat down on some crates near the fire, Wullie brought out a flask from under his cloak;

"Here's a wee dram tae wa'rm us up," he said, opening the flask.

Angus picked up a beaker and held it out, Wullie poured some whisky into it then held out the flask in a toast; "A guid New Year tae yae Angus an' monae o' them."

"An' the same tae yursel Wullie," the old man answered.

They drank their whisky and sat down.

Angus put a lump of coal on the fire, the flame caused their shadows to dance in the rafters far above their heads as they sat and chatted. He took another sip of whisky;

"Ah! That's a fine dram." The old man's face was aglow as he savoured the warm feeling as the liquid slipped down his throat and nestled in his stomach.

They sat quietly for a few minutes, and then Angus spoke again;

"Have yae heard aboot that wummin thit cam doon frae the heelans, ye ken, the wan thit's bidin wae auld Mrs Burns."

Wullie nodded but didn't speak.

"Well, ah hear she's awfae no' weel, an' her jist loosin' her man twa month since. It's that wee bairn Feea, ah feel sorry fur, he's only aboot fowr year ow'l an' if onythin' should happin' tae his maw thar'll be naebody tae look efter him."

Angus looked into the fire; "Ach, it's a damn shame fur the wee mite," he continued, shaking his head.

At that point Wullie silently nodded in agreement.

They sat and talked through the night, unaware of the drama that was unfolding in a quiet corner of the lower Stockwell.

# CAST OUT

In a dingy little room on the ground floor of an old tenement, a candle flickered. It sat on a small table near a bed where a woman was lying, gasping for breath. A small boy was standing next to her; his little hand gripped the bedclothes and started to shake them; "Mammy, me is hungry! Mammy, me is hungry!" he repeated anxiously.

Slowly, the woman raised her hand and placed it on her son's head. She spoke softly through laboured breath; "Hush, ma' wee lamb, hush, yer mammy's no weel an' she dinna hae onythin' fur yae".

The little boy started to sob; "Me is awfy hungry. Me wa'nts neeps, Mammy, me wa'nts neeps," he pleaded. The woman went into a fit of coughing and gasping, she grabbed the little boy's hand and held it tight as her body went into a spasm then, with a long drawn out sigh, her lifeless hand let go as it fell to the side of the bed. The room went silent as Feea stood with a puzzled look on his face. He took hold of his mother's hand and began to shake it;

"No seep, Mammy, wakey up...wakey up Mammy, no go seepy", there was a
sense of urgency in his voice, which soon turned to panic. He started shouting,
hysterically;

"Mammy no seep... Mammy no seep...Mammy wakey noo!"

He stopped and waited for a reaction, there was none; he started to shake her
frantically and screamed at the top of his voice; "Mammy! Mammy! Wakey up!
MAMMY!..." he screamed as tears streamed down his face.

His screaming and shouting brought the landlady to the door; she started
banging on it;

"Whit's gawn oan in ther'? Whit's a' this cummoshun in ma hoose?"

Feea continued screaming and shouting as the door opened. A large, rough
looking woman stood holding a lantern in the doorway. A profusion of black
hairs grew from a wart at the side of her chin. She staggered into the room,
obviously the worse for drink. Her long, black apron-covered skirt swept the
floor as she made her swaying way towards the centre of the sparsely furnished
room.

Feea ran over and pulled at her skirt, almost dragging her towards the bed;
"Wakey ma Mammy! Wakey ma Mammy!"He shouted, excitedly.

"Awricht! Awricht!" The woman growled as she put her hand out to support
herself against the wall. Then she staggered towards the bed and held up the
lantern. She looked down at the lifeless body of Feea's mother, her gaze
meeting that of the dead woman. She was gripped by a terror that soon changed
to anger as she mouthed the word; 'Plague'.

"You wakey ma Mammy noo," the little boy was still tugging at the woman's
skirt as he, innocently, looked up into her hate filled eyes. She put the lantern
down on the table beside the candle and grabbed a birch broom that was
standing against the wall.

She kicked the little boy away sending him sprawling to the floor. Feea
scrambled to his feet, pleading; "Wakey ma Ma..." he didn't get time to finish

the sentence, the broom came swishing down and caught him on the side of his head, the force sent him crashing against the wall.

"Yer maw, yer maw's deid, deid like yer faither, deid wae God knows whit. Noo, get oot ya wee brat! Get oot an' tak' yer disease wae yae, God scurse yae, an' yer faimily, fur bringing it tae ma hoose...Noo get oot! GET OOT!" the heartless bitch screeched.

Feea was screaming as he tried to get to his feet, the broom crashed down on his back again and again, as he tried to get to the door. The stinging twigs ripped and slashed his already ragged clothes and cut deep into his tender skin, taking his breath away with every searing stroke. The woman raised the broom high above her head as she went to continue her frenzied attack on the defenceless child. She brought the broom down in a sweeping arc but before it could make contact, she tripped on her long skirt and sent the broom crashing onto the lantern and candle that were on the table.

The lantern smashed, sending flaming oil across the floor and setting fire to her grease covered skirt. She screamed and dropped the broom.

Feea turned his head, and, seeing the screaming woman engulfed in flames, scrambled to his feet, and ran out the door into the foggy street.

He ran into the murk with the terrifying sound of the woman's screams, ringing in his ears.

He ran through closes, down lanes and through filthy, garbage-strewn alleys, in his panic-stricken flight from the scene of unspeakable horror.

With his heart pounding in his chest, he ran into an alley that had tall tenement buildings on either side. Half way down the alley, his toe stubbed a cobble and sent him flying into a pile of garbage stacked against a wall.

There was a 'yelp' as a scruffy little mongrel puppy scrambled out from under the pile. It scampered down the alley then stopped and looked back at the little boy extricating himself from the pile of rubbish.

Feea sat down with his head in his hands and started to cry, the little dog watched for a few minutes then, hesitating every few feet, started to crawl along the side of the wall towards him. When it had gained enough courage and realised that there was no danger, the little dog came and sat at Feea's feet. It tilted its head to the side, and looked up with sad, puzzled eyes at the sobbing boy.

High above them, a warm glow came from some of the windows.

There was the sound of singing and laughter as the tenants celebrated in their cosy surroundings. Feea looked up, longingly, towards the world that he had been cast out of, and at that moment, realised that he was utterly alone.

He felt something touch his leg and on looking down saw the little puppy looking up with mournful eyes. He reached down; the little dog licked his hand as it recognised a kindred spirit.

He stroked its head, and, in the dark shadows of that alley, an invisible bond was sealed between two lonely wretches, who had been abandoned in the tempest of life.

Feea picked up an old sack and wrapped it round his shoulders in an effort to protect himself from the bitter cold. He then got up, and with his mind in turmoil, slowly made his way down the alley, closely followed by the little dog. Snow began to fall, and as they made their silent way, they left a little trail in the snow that would soon vanish, unobserved, into oblivion.

The snow was getting heavier as they wandered along the dark, deserted streets. The singing died away as the revellers in the tenements retired for the night, and one by one the windows darkened as candles and lamps were extinguished.

They turned into a street off the Gallowgate and the little dog ran ahead. It stopped at a wooden building and started to scratch at one of the boards on the wall. The little dog was very excited as it pawed and snarled at it. There was a flurry of snow as it tried to burrow at the bottom of the wooden plank where it met the ground. Feea went over to see what the little dog was so excited about. When he touched the board, it moved. Being held on with only one nail, it swung like a pendulum.

Feea pushed it to the side revealing an entrance to the building.

The little dog went inside followed by Feea. Although it was very dark and a bit scary, it was dry and a lot warmer than outside.

The little boy peered into the gloom until his eyes became more accustomed to the dark.

He saw a pile of straw in the corner next to the loose board.

The little dog was jumping about on it and causing the straw to fly in all directions.

Feea went inside, made his way over to the straw and sat down. The little dog curled up beside him.

Feea held him close as he nervously listened to the strange sounds that seemed to be all around them.

There was the tapping on cobbles, the sound of rubbing against creaking posts and the occasional snort. He pulled some straw over himself and the little dog and they both fell asleep.

Feea's dreams were a confusion of reality and fantasy.

It was as if he was caught up in a whirlpool, and was going round and round as it sucked him downward.

The scenes of all that had happened to him that day became all jumbled up and were tumbling into a black cauldron at the spiralling centre.

He tossed and turned; much to the annoyance of the little dog, then he fell into a deep sleep and settled down.

## MACGURK'S STABLE

It was New Year's morning and Andy MacGurk was suffering from the mother and father of all hangovers as he made his way along the Gallowgate. The clock in the Tollbooth was striking seven and every 'DONG' from the bell reverberated round the inside of his throbbing head as he turned into the street where his stable was situated. The crunch of his boots in the crisp snow echoed from the nearby tenements as he made his unsteady way down the deserted street. He tucked his scarf into his jacket and pulled his hat down over his ears as he approached the gate to the stable yard. A wind got up and blew the powdery snow into spiralling circles that haphazardly danced around the street and caused a few flakes to settle on his red, bulbous nose. A nose as he would tell anyone, who made a comment about it, had cost him a pretty penny in the inns and taverns around town. He was in his sixties and had been a carter all his life. Although there was no work for the horses, he was going in to check that they were all right and do a little stable work while he was there. He loved his horses and, as on many occasions Peggy his wife would make the comment that, he thought more of them than he did of her. He always answered her by making the ill-advised observation that they looked better than she did. That always went down well, and resulted in him having to duck a flying pot or pan as he made a hasty retreat out the door on his way to a safe haven, which usually was the nearest tavern. He could rely on dinner being cancelled on those occasions and a verbal assault on his eardrums when he finally staggered back full of 'Dutch courage', less than sincere apologies, and fortified with the strong influences of John Barleycorn. Now that is a precarious combination especially when confronting an irate wife who is not only twice your weight and a head taller but she can stand on her feet while you struggle to stay on yours. That's bad enough but at the same time; you are trying to make the words that you are thinking come out in the right order and failing miserably. On those occasions old Andy would, somehow, stagger to his bed through a barrage of curses, declarations and profundities, and escape into the sanctuary of drunken oblivion. It had been like that the previous evening and he could still hear his wife's morning sermon ringing in his ears.

He drew the bolt and pushed the wooden sparred gate open. It creaked, as it swung inward, leaving a rutted arc in the snow.

He entered the yard, made his way over to the stable, and went inside. When his eyes had adjusted to the dark surroundings, he crossed over to the far wall and, with fumbling fingers struck a match and lit a lantern.

There were six horses in the stable, all Clydesdales. His favourite was Bella the bay-chestnut mare. Old Bella had seen him through many a tight squeeze in more ways than one. She had been with him since she was a foal and now, even though she was nearing the end of her working career, she could still pull a fully laden cart up High street, where some of the other horses would be struggling. Andy went over to Bella's stall and gave her a friendly pat on the neck. The old mare showed her appreciation by making snorting noises and stamping her hoof on the cobbled floor of her stall. This attracted the attention of the other horses who popped their heads over the stall doors and started nodding up and down as if to attract Andy's attention. "A guid New Year tae ye a'!" he called out and immediately paid the price of his exuberance with a sharp throbbing pain in his head. He sat down on an upturned bucket and with his head in his hands waited until the throbbing pain subsided. There was a whoosh as one of the horses relieved itself, sending a puff of steam up into the cold air. This brought Andy's attention back to the job at hand, but first, getting his priorities in order, he reached into his back pocket and brought out a flask. He took a drink from it and with a deep drawn out sigh, replaced the top and gave his head a shake; "Ah, that's better," he said to himself and got up feeling more refreshed. It wasn't so much 'the hair of the dog that bit him' as 'the hair of the dog that savaged him' the previous evening.

Having tied an old sack around his waist, he started to clean out the stalls. Once he had finished the first one, he went over to the corner to get some fresh straw. He was just about to dig his pitchfork into it when he saw the straw move. Gingerly he used the pitchfork to draw back the straw and was surprised to see the little dog staring up at him with its big sad eyes, as it lay beside Feea who was fast asleep. The little dog looked terrified as it looked up at the man towering above him, holding his pitchfork at the ready. The old man had unwittingly adopted the threatening pose of a gladiator standing with his trident ready for the kill. He was an awesome sight, especially with him being unshaven, unwashed, and trying to recover from a hangover.

His attitude softened as he looked on the pitiful sight of the little boy lying in the straw. "Pair wee mite, ah wunner how he gote in here?" he thought to himself. He reached down and clapped the little dog that cowered in closer to Feea. He looked around and saw the loose board hanging slightly to the side; "This must be how they gote in, I always meant to fix that. Maybe it's jist as weel thit ah didnae. The pair wee bairn wid'ave frozen tae death oot there." He pushed the board back into place and replaced the straw over Feea and the little dog. "Yer no dae'n ony herm layin' ther," he thought to himself, and, picking up some straw with the pitchfork, carried it over to the stall and continued with his chores. When he had finished, he left Feea sleeping and went home. He returned a little later carrying some scraps of food wrapped up in a piece of linen and a jug of milk.

When he entered the stable, Feea was sitting up and rubbing his eyes while the little dog was sniffing around near the stalls. When it saw Andy it ran over to where Feea was sitting and crouched down with its front paws outstretched looking in the direction of the approaching man. Feea looked apprehensive, as Andy got closer.

"Me no dae nuthin', mister," he almost pleaded.

"Och that's a' richt laddie, a've broat ye sumthin' tae eat," the old carter said with a smile and handed the little bundle to the cowering boy. Feea opened it and started to munch into the pieces of meat and oatcakes, almost choking as he filled his mouth.

"Tak' it easy laddie there's plenty there fur you an' yer wee dug," Andy said with a smile. The little dog started yelping when it smelled the food. Feea threw it some pieces of meat and the two of them ate heartily. Feea had never tasted anything so good. The old man sat down on his bucket and watched them eating as if it was the last food on Earth. He got up and crossed over to a bench where he picked up a beaker and a tin plate. He gave them a wipe then poured some milk in them and took them over to where the two companions were dining. He put the plate on the ground and handed the beaker to Feea, who gulped the milk down so fast that it made him cough and splutter and left the form of a white moustache above his top lip. He laughed when he looked down and found that he had covered the little dog in milk. It was looking up in surprise as the milk dripped from its nose.

Andy burst out laughing as well when he saw the little dog's face.

He playfully rubbed it's head;

"Och yer nuthin' bit a wee scruff," he said jokingly.

"Him Scruff?" Feea asked with a quizzical look on his face.

"Weel it's as gid a name as onay," the old man answered, nodding his head.

"Me ca' him Scruff tae, then," Feea said and continued eating. Andy left them alone and got on with mucking out the stables.

This was how Feea and his little dog started out on the streets of Glasgow.

# THE ART OF SURVIVAL.

One day, when Feea was about 5 years old, he sat down on rock near the Nelson Monument in Glasgow Green. He hadn't eaten for a few days and was really hungry. As he sat listening to his stomach rumbling his attention was drawn to some birds acting strangely; they seemed to be stamping their feet on the ground in a kind of dance, Feea watched as the birds bent down and pulled worms from the grass and ate them. He got up and as soon as he made his way towards them; they flew off. He looked down at the ground and was amazed to see dozens of worms wriggling about. He picked one up and watched it wriggle between his fingers. While he gazed at it he felt the hunger pangs in his stomach, to his simple mind, if the birds ate them then they must be food and his stomach was screaming out for food. So without hesitation he popped it into his mouth and ate it. At first the taste was rather strange but not unpleasant so he swallowed it and bent down for another one, this one was bigger and wriggled about in his mouth, he giggled at the strange feeling on his tongue, this one tasted better than the last so he gobbled it down and picked up another; he had found food in the most unlikely of places and this episode probably saved his life. On a dull, overcast day Feea would mimic the birds and turned their actions into a kind of dance that he made his own; a dance that kept him nourished in times when there was no food to be found. But when it rained and especially during a thunderstorm, he would be seen running up and down the streets in a kind of frenzy, as he grabbed all the worms that he could see in the pools and puddles. On these occasions he was in his glory. As obnoxious as it may sound Feea had found a source of high protein purely by accident and at the same time, and without realising it had found a way of earning coins on the street with his unique way of dancing. It was around this time, that while doing his little dance on the back green of an inn one night, he heard singing and without realizing it, he started dancing to the rhythm of the music; the song was 'Killiecrankie' and it remained as his favourite. From that night he would dance where ever and whenever he heard music or singing and when it was on the streets, the passers-by would throw him coins, usually halfpennies or pennies; if he was quick enough he would grab them before they were picked up by some other urchin or beggar nearby. Many of the buskers appreciated the boost in business that Feea brought with his flamboyant dances and shared the money with him, but there were others who kept the money and left him sitting at the side of the pavement; Feea didn't mind he enjoyed the dance anyway.

It was a year or two later and in a more elegant part of the city, that he learned another trait that was to become a part of his manner. Feea had made a habit of wandering the lanes that ran along the back of the elegant houses. These houses were an exact contrast to the squalor of the lower class residences. They were large mansions with winding driveways and had there own private stables where they kept the horses that pulled their highly polished carriages. The resident families were attended by a large staff of servants which ranged from the housekeeper right down to the scullery-maid. They were mostly of Scottish decent, except for one or two who were of African origin; either ex-slaves or the descendents of slaves. This was a world far apart from the one that Feea was used to. But to his mind, people were people; he knew nothing about 'classes', whether it be upper or lower, everyone was equal; only age made the difference. From his observations of the grown-ups that he had come into contact with, they were on the whole friendly and tolerant but they could be dangerous when annoyed. Feea noticed that they would rather watch than play, while on the other hand the younger population saw everything as a game, a game that they had to take part in and Feea loved to play, especially if it entailed running or jumping. At this kind of game he became a true 'champion' and when you consider his, sometimes, obnoxious diet, you could say that, he was 'King of the Cannibal Islands' in more ways than one. He was barely seven years old when he made these excursions to this part of the town and it was here that, on observation, he learned one of his mannerisms that put him above his peers. He had a habit of climbing up on the garden walls where he would sit quietly and watch the goings-on in the mansion grounds; mostly the staff would ignore him. But on one or two occasions he was chased away; especially when the master or mistress of that particular house was about. On many occasions he had noticed the way that the servants reacted in the presence of their masters, in particular the way they bowed before them and on occasion, kissed their hands, especially if they had received a gift or favour. Feea made this his method of showing his appreciation to others for kind acts towards him, only he took it a stage further and adopted the stance that a 'Dandy' would take on introducing himself to a lady; this trait stayed with him all his life.

It was two years later, that the first monument to Admiral Lord Nelson to be erected anywhere in Britain was being constructed on Glasgow Green. Feea wandered down to see what was going on and was amazed at the huge monolith that could be seen through the wooden scaffolding that surrounded its massive structure. He sat on the grass, watching the workmen as they went about their numerous tasks and marvelled at how some of the men could throw a tool up to a workmate high up on the structure. He came every day and sat, cross-legged, on the grass with his eyes glued to the huge pinnacle as it took shape. Some of the men were bemused to see this little urchin sitting there every day and during their break would throw him a bit of their lunch that Feea retrieved by using some goal-keeping antics that caused some of the men to break into rapturous applause.

One day, just after their break, one of the men dropped a chisel as he climbed the scaffold. As it tumbled through the structure, Feea jumped to his feet and ran over shouting, "Me get it! Me get it!" He picked up the tool and, taking a few steps back, threw it as hard as he could in the direction of the workman, who was half-way up the scaffold, it landed on a platform beside him. The man picked it up and shouted down to Feea.

"Thanks laddie, yer a braw wee pitcher," then he continued his climb to the upper platform. One of the men working on the ground, crossed over to Feea; he appeared to be the foreman.

"Where did yae learn tae dae that," he asked, with a broad grin on his face.

"Och, me wis watchin' the mannies daein' it awe the time," Feea answered; the man smiled.

"Bit that's an awfae lang wie up fur a wee lad like you tae be able tae throw," the man said, pointing up to where the chisel had landed.

"Och, Feea kin toss it higher thin that," Feea said, nodding his head.

"Who is Feea?" the man asked.

"Me is Feea," the little lad answered with a smile.

"Oh, a see," the man smiled back. He turned to a pile of small rocks that had been left over from the foundations, some of which had been brought from the lower reaches of the Clyde and were very smooth. He picked one up that was almost spherical and had a white streak that went all the way round, making it look as if the two halves had been stuck together.

"Whit dae ye think o' that?" he said handing it to Feea.

"Oh, it's braw," Feea answered, rubbing the stone on his sleeve.

"Well let me see how high ye kin throw it, bit keep it awa frae the Monument," the man said pointing to the sky with his back to the construction.

Feea stood, rubbing the stone on his sleeve, and then he took aim and fired it up into the sky. He stood for a second or two, watching it get smaller as it climbed, then he took off like a hare and still keeping his eye on the stone, caught it before it came back down to the ground. The man stood with his mouth open in utter amazement; he had never seen anything like this before. When Feea came back with the stone, he looked up at the man who was still standing with his mouth open and looking out into space.

"Wis that awe richt mister," he said with a daft look on his face. Slowly the man lowered his gaze and shaking his head, spoke slowly and deliberately.

"Where did ye learn tae dae that."

"Och, me an' some o' the boyes play at chuckin' stanes ower the river tae see wha kin get maste o' thum oan the ither side, it gid fun an' me is the champion," he said pushing out his chest and standing with his hands on his waist.

"Naebody'll believe this," the man said to himself. They sat down on the grass and looked towards the Monument. The man was deep in thought as he stared at the three-quarter built construction, then he turned to Feea.

"Dae ye think ye kin toss that stane ower that?" he said pointing at the partly constructed monolith.

"Och aye me kin dae that awe richt," Feea answered, getting to his feet. The man pulled him back down.

"Naw no' jist noo, wait tae efter work an' then ye kin show the ither men whit ye kin dae."

Feea nodded his head in agreement and sat down again.

"You hing aboot here an' a'll see ye efter," the man said as he got up and went back to where he had been working.

After work, the men gathered in a group at the side of the construction. The man that had been talking to Feea was standing in the middle and every now and than would point in Feea's direction, when he did this the other man shook their heads. Then they reached into there pockets and handed coins to the foreman. He signalled for Feea to come over.

Feea got up and crossed over to the mumbling men.

"Show the men the stane," the foreman said to Feea. Feea held out the stone so that they all could see it.

"Nae chance, it's too big, a fu'lly grown man couldnae dae it," one of the men said and others agreed.

"An' yae say he'll catch it own the ither side," came a voice from the back.

"Aye," the foreman answered.

"In that case, A'll go doubles," one of the men said, handing some more coins to the foreman.

"The foreman turned to Feea.

"Awe richt, laddie, dae yer stuff. As Feea got ready to throw the stone, some of the men shouted.

"Wait tae we get roon tae the ither side, jist in case there is ony jiggery-pokery," and with that five of the men ran round to the other side of the construction.

"Awe rich ," came a shout from the other side.

Feea rubbed the stone on his sleeve, took aim then let it fly. The men stood with their mouths gaping as they watched the stone go higher and higher until it disappeared over the top. By this time Feea was off and running round to the back, where he jumped and caught the stone right in front of the disbelieving workmen. The rest of the men came round and with the look on their workmate's faces, knew that Feea had done it. The foreman was beaming as he slapped Feea on the back.

"Weel done laddie," then he turned to the other men "A telt ye didn't a. He's a wee marvel, that's whit he is, a wee marvel." The men agreed. The foreman pulled Feea aside and pressed four pennies into his hand.

"Take this laddie an' hod oan tae that stane; it's a lucky wan fur yae."

"Aye it be ma 'lucky chuckie'," Feea answered, putting the stone in his pocket. From that day on he treasured it and never let anyone touch it.

As the weeks passed he got friendly with the men and would run messages for them in exchange for a share in their lunch. When the monument was finished and the opening ceremony had passed, Feea would be seen running and dancing round the great structure as if he had built it himself, on other occasions he would be seen, sitting gazing at it; to him, this was the 'eighth wonder of the world', or in his world, the only wonder.

Most Sundays Feea would be seen at the top of Queen Street where the Ewing mansion stood. This elegant house was surrounded with tall trees where the crows nested; to the inhabitants of Glasgow it was known as 'The Rookery'. This was one of Feea's favourite places. Here he could be seen waiving his arms and mimicking the birds in flight, every now and then he would leap into the air in his vane attempt to join them, but alas that was their domain and he had to be content with the pretence of flying on the ground; but it didn't stop him from trying non the less. Once he tired of this, he would wander down to Glassford Street and sit, mumbling to himself, at the edge of the pavement, outside the Trades Hall. After his monogamous conversation, he would get to his feet and, although he couldn't fly, he could certainly leap and with one bound, he would jump across Glassford Street from one pavement to the other and back again. The street was narrower then but even so, no other boy in all of Glasgow could match this great feat or the fact that he could run the length of Argyle Street, from Glasgow Cross to St Enoch's Square, in less than two minutes. These achievements put him above all others and they in turn showed respect for his abilities. They may have laughed and giggled at his, sometimes bizarre, traits but they envied his athletic prowess.

Feea had many weird and wonderful ideas, one of which was, when he was about seven or eight years old. When they had bedded down for the night, he used to tie a piece of twine round Scruff's neck and tie the other end to his big toe; just in case the little dog should try to wander off in the night and leave Feea without the heat from its body. This worked all right, that is until one Monday morning in the middle of summer.

The night before had been very warm and muggy, so Feea decided to sleep under a tree on the Green. In the middle of the night there had been a shower which left little pools of water scattered about. But being under the tree he had stayed dry. It was about six-o-clock in the morning when Maxi Black went to open the gates of the slaughter-house at the Flesher's Haugh. He had no sooner opened the padlock, when it and the chain went crashing on to the cobbled ground. The clatter caused a large rat to scamper out of the yard and into the Green. As it scurried past Feea, who was fast asleep, it caught the attention of Scruff, who instinctively took off in pursuit. Feea screamed as he was dragged from his slumber in the most undignified manner. Meanwhile, Wullie Balornock was coming to the end of his shift and had sat down on a rock enjoying his pipe. He looked over to see what all the commotion was and burst out laughing when he saw Feea sitting in a pool of muddy water, trying to get the twine off his toe while Scruff was trying to pull him further in and in its excited state was kicking back a shower of mud that covered his protesting and very irate master as it attempted to get at the rat. Wullie shook his head. "It could only be Feea," he said to himself then burst out laughing again as he went over to help the little lad get out of the predicament that he had found himself in. That was the last time that Feea tried that stunt.

# TRADES HALL

It was Saturday night on the twenty- seventh of November, the night of the annual ball in the Trades Hall in Glassford Street. Inside the main hall was an array of bunting and splendour. Every one was dressed in their finest attire. The young boys looked almost regimental in their black long-tail coats, black silk knee breaches, white silk ruffled shirts and highly polished shoes. They were in the exact mimic of their father's formal attire. The young girls were positively in bloom as they posed in their prettiest, long, hooped gowns. They stood in little groups giggling and giving the occasional glance in the direction of the boys who were standing, fidgeting and wishing that they could be somewhere else. The mothers were casting admiring glances at their offspring in the self-assured knowledge that their progenies outshone all the others. The fathers looked the epitome of total boredom as they stood around, almost panting for a good cigar and a glass of port. The whole place was awash with colour and the sound of girlish frivolity and last minute titillation as the heady aroma of the many posies and pomanders drifted up towards the polished rafters, high above their heads. Amidst all this gentility and splendour stood, what could only be described as a positive, pouting peacock in the shape of the dance master, one, Cedric Pilkington-Blythe. He was a tall, lanky individual wearing a powdered wig and had a powdered face complete with a black beauty spot to go with it. He wore a white silk tailcoat with matching knee breaches, a pink, fluffed up, ruffled shirt with dainty frills for cuffs. A large pomander hung from his left wrist and in his right hand he held a long silver tipped cane that he used in a swaying motion as he strutted, almost ballet like from one little group to another. His strutting shadow danced amidst the others as he passed the myriad of candelabra that lined the walls. The members of the string quartet were tuning their instruments as they sat in the musician's gallery at the far end of the hall. When he had finished fraternizing with those, that to his pompous mind were merely plebeians and therefore far below, his, self- exalted station, the Dance Master made his majestic way up the centre of the hall. He cleared a path through the chattering throng with the mere flick of a silk handkerchief that was hanging from his limp wrist as if he was warding off some irritating insects. With head held high, he smugly looked down his long pointed nose at, as he would like them to believe, his subjects. They, in deference, yielded to his unhindered progress. On reaching his podium, he cast a glance in the direction of the musician's gallery. With a bow of their heads and a nod to each other, the quartet prepared to start. With one tap of his cane, the room fell silent. The Dance Master cast an approving smirk at his obedient audience before announcing that the first dance would be a chanteuse performed by the children of his 'Academe d' Danse'. He tapped his cane again. The mothers and fathers lined the sides of the hall as their children took up their positions in the centre of the floor. With a cold, expressionless gaze, Pilkington-Blythe looked down his nose at his young prodigies. God forbid that they would put a foot wrong or mistimed a curtsy or bow, for their backsides bore witness to the wrath of their tutor. He tapped his cane again; the girls curtsied in front of their partners and they in turn bowed gracefully, then with a double tap of the cane, the quartet came to life. The mothers watched with excited admiration as their children glided across the floor with such elegance.

Meanwhile, down on the street Feea was sitting at the edge of the pavement talking to himself. He had just finished rummaging through the dungsteads in the lane and was covered in filth of every description. He was unbreached, the only thing he had on was an old ragged shirt and his feet were caked in mud. His ears picked up the sound of music drifting down from the building behind him. He turned round in the direction of the sweet sounds and his head started to sway from side to side in time to the rhythm. He got up and started to dance in circles on the pavement but on seeing the unattended door, followed the sound, Pied Piper fashion, into the building and up the stairs. The doors to the main hall on the first floor were closed; Feea started dancing on the landing outside them. He pranced and twirled but his over exuberance in a pirouette sent him into an uncontrollable spin towards the hall doors and with a mighty crash, burst in. He landed on his bare backside right in the middle of the dancers. If a nest of rats followed by a pack of snarling dogs had burst into that room, the result would have been the same. In that moment Feea had turned a scene of serenity and elegance into a complete shambles: chaos reigned supreme. Girls were screaming, mothers were fainting and little Molly Simpson wet her self when she saw Feea sprawled on the floor at her feet. The floor soon cleared leaving Feea sitting up and looking around at the confusion all around him. Some of the fathers were holding their hands over their mouths to keep them from bursting into bellows of laughter.

Pilkington –Blythe stood on his podium, fuming. His face was getting redder and redder as he glowered at the disgusting little reprobate who had invaded his well organized ensemble and had dispatched all his weeks of sweating, planning and vigorous preparation, into the dustbin. He made his move. Feea turned when he heard the click, click, clicking of the cane coming down the hall behind him and when he saw the Dance Master, looking for all the world like The Grim Reaper bearing down on him, he sprang to his feet and bounded out the door and down the stairs. When he ran out into the street the boys who knew him started to shout from the windows;

"A ham for Feea! A ham for Feea!" they called, (meaning a worm).

Feea by this time had made his escape into the Trongate. He ran along the street until he got to the Tollbooth, there he sat down with his back against the wall and caught his breath; while casting the occasional glance back towards Glassford Street; just in case he had been followed.

As he sat looking up at the sky, he heard Scruff's familiar yelp coming from a backcourt across the street. He got up and went over to investigate.

When he entered the backcourt, he called the little dog's name. There was the sound of a scuffle, then two shapes came bounding out of the darkness and pushed him on his back as they made their escape through the close with Scruff hard on their heels. Feea dived like a goalkeeper and grabbed the little dog as it ran passed him. He held it tight as it tried to escape.

"No run efter the bad mannies," he said as he clapped the little dog and calmed it down. His attention was drawn to the sound of moaning coming from a dark corner of the backcourt. He put the dog down and no sooner had its paws touched the ground than it was off.

Being very cautious, Feea went over to investigate the sounds coming from the corner. He peered into the darkness and saw the large, motionless shape of a man huddled on the ground. He bent down to give him a shake but he had no sooner touched him than the big man turned. His rough hand grabbed Feea by the scruff of the neck and dragged him down onto the ground. Feea tried to speak but he couldn't, due to the fact that the point of a dagger was prodding his throat.

"Me no dae nuthin'! Me nn…no dae nuthin'!" He stammered. "Me only come ower tae get Scruff."

"Och it's you Feea." The man let go and got to his feet. He groaned and sat down with his back against the wall, holding his shoulder.

Feea recognized the man when he saw him in the moonlight. It was Mungo MacNab the blacksmith.

Mungo worked hard at his trade, but he was also a fence for stolen goods and mixed with the undesirables that hung around the town.

Being a hard man to deal with, he made many enemies; two of them had attacked him that night.

"Did ye see who it wis?" He asked Feea, who was looking at him with a worried expression on his face.

"Naw, me no see thum, it wus too dork," he answered, taking a hesitant step backward. Mungo rubbed his shoulder and groaned.

Feea noticed some blood dripping from the sleeve of the blacksmith's jacket.

"Ur ye a' richt, Mistur Mungo?" He said, pointing to the man's arm. Mungo tried to stand upright but the effort caused him to sway and stagger back against the wall.

"A'll be aw richt if ye help me back tae the forge; kin yae dae that fur me?" He said, rubbing his arm. Feea nodded and went over to the blacksmith.

They made their way out of the backcourt and onto the Saltmarket, stopping every few paces so that Mungo could catch his breath and muster the strength to go on, as he was in a weak state due to the amount of blood that he had lost. Eventually, they arrived at the smithy, which was situated at the corner of Clyde Street, almost opposite the Custom Shed on the docks.

When they got inside, Mungo got Feea to help him over to the forge, which had a slight glow from its dying embers. An old oil lamp sat flickering on top of a barrel beside the anvil and beside it was a pile of tools. Using Feea for support he went over and rummaged through the pile of iron implements. He picked up a long poker and went back to the forge where, with great effort,   pushed the tip of the rod into the heart of the glowing cinders, and then he prodded the end of a set of bellows into the char.

The effort caused him to sway and fall towards the forge; Feea grabbed him in time and pulled him back. He helped him over to a crate near the anvil there the blacksmith planted himself down, almost in a state of collapse. He turned to Feea,

"We dinna' hae much time lad, A'm nearly done fur. Pump the bellows till the poker's rid hote, then ye'll hive tae hod it oan the wound oan ma shooder tae stope the blood." Feea looked at him with disbelief,

"Bit that wull be auffy sare, Mr Mungo," he said with shocked concern in his voice.

Mungo grabbed the boy's arm and looked him straight in the eye,

"If yea dinna dae that fur me, A'll be deed pretty soon, yea must dae it fur me, Feea, yea hiv tae, its ma only chance; we hiv tae stope the bleedin' or A'm done fur." He put a little stone bottle on the anvil. "When ye've done that pour some o' that liniment oan it tae stope it festurn; noo get oan the end o' thae bellows." Feea did as Mungo said and started to pump the bellows till the coals and the end of the poker got 'white hot'.

Mungo pulled his jacket and shirt off, exposing the deep wound at the back of his shoulder. Blood was pouring from the gash and was running down his back. He put his hand into his jacket pocket and brought out a flask, containing whiskey, he took the top off, and, holding in his right hand, called over to Feea. "It'll be ready noo, grab it wae a rag an' bring it ower." Feea picked up a dirty piece of cloth and pulled the glowing poker from the forge. He held it with both hands and went over to where Mungo was sitting. The blacksmith turned his back to Feea. The little lad let out a gasp when he saw the wound and the amount of blood that was pouring from it. Mungo turned his head to the side. "When I tell yea, ho'd the end o' the poker oan the wound tae it stopes bleedin'. Ur yea ready?"

"Bit... its gonnae be awfae sare," Feea stammered.

"Dinnna you worry aboot that, jist dae it when a tell yea,ur yea ready?" The big man said with a degree of urgency in his voice.

"Awe right", Feea answered nervously.

Mungo took two long gulps of whiskey and put the flask down on the floor beside him.

"Dae it noo," he gasped.

"B..but", Feea stammered.

"Dae it noo!" Mungo shouted.

Feea held the glowing poker above the wound, grimaced, closed his eyes, then pressed it down onto the blood spurting cavity. There was a sizzling sound as it touched the flesh.

Mungo let out a scream and with instinctive reaction, turned and with one swift movement, landed his huge fist right on Feea's chin. The impact lifted the little lad off his feet and with the poker clanging onto the stone floor, sent him flying across the workshop where he landed unconscious, in a heap in the corner. Mungo, on realising what he had done, tried to get to his feet and go over to where Feea was lying but the excruciating pain acted like a fuse blowing in his head. He dropped to his knees and fell forward into oblivion. The only sound that was heard to disturb the eerie silence in the workshop was the occasional spark from the dying embers in the forge.

Feea was first to recover. The workshop seemed to be spinning as he sat up, he didn't know whether to rub the lump that he had received on the back of his head, when he hit the floor, or the throbbing in his chin; where Mungo had hit him. He looked over and saw the big blacksmith lying face down in the middle of the floor. He went over and knelt down beside him.

"Mistur Mungo, ur yae awe richt,' he said, shaking the big man, making sure that he didn't touch his shoulder; just in case he should get another thump on the chin. After a few moments, Mungo began to stir. He groaned then turned and sat up. There was a bruised lump on his forehead; an injury that he received when he hit the cobbled floor. He reached out and grabbed the flask of whisky that he had left on the floor, near the anvil and after taking a long swallow, let out a sigh.

"Ah! That's better, that's the best pain killer o' thum awe," he uttered breathlessly. When he had composed himself he addressed Feea.

"Och, am awfy sorry aboot biffin yae oan the jaw lad, it's a natural reaction wae me; ur yae awe richt?"

"Aye, bit ma jaw is awfae sair; me gote noakayed oot," Feea answered; rubbing his jaw.

"A think 'me gote noakayed oot' as weel," the blacksmith answered; mimicking Feea. He tried to laugh but the effort caused a sharp pain to shoot through his shoulder; he thought better of it and forced a smile instead.

"Yer a guid lad an' ye've done me a gid service this nicht; wan thit A'll no furget." Painfully, he got to his feet and staggered over to the workbench. Feea watched as Mungo fumbled among a pile of old rags. After a few seconds, he pulled out a stone flask.

"Ah, ther yae ur," he sighed. He took the flask and staggered over to a dirty old wooden bed at the back of the workshop; there he planted himself down with such force that Feea thought it was going to collapse.

"You gang awa noo, laddie 'cause am gonnae get fu' an' kip doon here." He made a gesture with his hand for Feea to come over.

Gingerly the little lad went over to the bed; Mungo gestured for him to come closer. As Feea stepped forward, Mungo grabbed him by the collar and pulling him down, spoke right into his ear.

"If onybody ever gees yae ony trouble you tell me an A'll fix thum fur yae; awe richt, yer ma wee pal noo an' A'll look oot fur yae, dinnae furget that." He let Feea go, giving him a playful slap on the back of the head. "Noo dinnae furget that, dae yae hear," he added pointing at Feea.

"Naw me wullnae," Feea answered, as he made his way out of the workshop; he was relieved to get away. He made his way to his secret place in McGurks stable, picking up Scruff on the way; it had been a very eventful evening and he was glad to get back to the comparatively peaceful company of the old Clydesdales.

## WILLIE 'THE WEASEL'

The cell door clanked shut.  The jailer turned the key in the lock and looked in at
the prisoner pushing his way through his cell- mates as he made his way over to
the barred window.  He, arrogantly, pulled an old man away from the window
and sent him sprawling on the floor.  Then he just stood there, gazing out into
the street.

"Hae a guid look Weasel, it's a' thit you'll be seein' fur a while," the jailer said
sarcastically.

"Och, awa an' bile yer can," the prisoner grunted without turning round.

This was Wullie Borland, better known as 'Wullie the Weasel', an evil
reprobate who was a frequent visitor to his present accommodation.

Wullie had come to Glasgow from Ayrshire, where, no doubt he would have
been wanted for some crime or other.  He was the youngest son in a family of
five.  His two elder brothers had been transported not long after their father had
been hung for murdering a judge near Tarbolton.  Wullie continued in the family
tradition of being an evil little scoundrel.  He got the nickname of 'The Weasel'
due to his small, slender stature, dirty red hair and vicious character.  He was a
master pickpocket, cat burglar, grave robber and all round criminal.  No crime

was too low for Wullie, and that included murder.

He had an annoying habit of looking over your shoulder and speaking into your ear from the corner of his mouth when he wanted to tell you something; it was advisable to check ones pockets after having a conversation with The Weasel. He wore a battered stovepipe hat and carried a stiletto dagger in the pocket of his dirty long coat. His scraggly, red hair was partially hidden by a scarf, or muffler, that also served as a weapon when the occasion called for it.

His partner in crime was a tall, heavily built, red-faced Irishman called Malky Monachan. Malky was the epitome of the saying 'all brawn and no brains'. He had huge callused hands and broad shoulders. The big Irishman worked on the wharf for a while but that job didn't last very long. He didn't quite understand that he was supposed to stack the goods, not help himself to them. That 'partnership' was dissolved when his employers found out, causing Malky to take up residence in the' House of Bars' for a while. It was there that he met 'The Weasel'. They shared a cell on the first floor of the prison. When Wullie saw the build of the Irishman and the extent of his intellect, he realised that he would make the perfect partner in the pick-pocketing profession. They made a formidable team; 'The Devil's Duo'. No one was safe from this pair whether alive or dead, for their crimes went beyond the grave. On this occasion, Malky was lucky enough to escape from the scene of the crime; a little matter of relieving a poor old lady of her money pouch, which had a mere pittance inside. Wullie, on the other hand, had made the mistake of not looking behind, if he had, he would have seen Black Jock watching him from the corner. Wullie had no sooner lifted the old woman's pouch, when, he felt an almighty thud on the back of his head, followed by the sensation of falling into a black, swirling fog. Jock's cudgel had done its work in the hands of an expert and the burly policeman was certainly that. By the time Wullie had recovered, he was in custody and the old woman had her meagre possessions back. So the Tollbooth was to be Wullie's abode until his appearance in court the next morning. The cell was overcrowded with petty thieves, drunkards, debtors and a few characters whose mental state was open to question. As there was no form of sanitation, the stench was overpowering and the only escape from the vile smell was over at the barred window. The inmates were treated no better than animals in a cage. Once a day they were given stale bread and water. This was all that they had to survive on, unless a relative or friend would bring some extra food. In the Weasel's case, this was highly unlikely as he was, to say the least, very short on both. But he survived the ordeal by threatening those who were lucky enough to have some food sent in. They would rather share it with the Weasel than have to watch their backs when they got out. Wullie soon took control of the cell and picked the best place to sleep. In the morning he was brought before the Magistrate and sentenced to twenty–eight days in the Tollbooth; so The Weasel was taken away and bundled back into the cell again. He cursed his luck as he looked out of the window and envied the ordinary townsfolk going about their business down in the street. From his cell window he could look right down the Saltmarket as far as the old wooden bridge over the Clyde. He cursed when he saw Wullie and Jock standing at the corner of Saltmarket and the Trongate. The two policemen were keeping a watchful eye out for any potential pickpockets or troublemakers as the shoppers mingled around the shops and stalls near the Cross.

Wullie turned from the window and sat down on some straw; soon he would be back out to continue his evil lifestyle among the unsuspecting citizens of Glasgow.

# THE DRAGON

Robert Dreghorn was a middle-aged man who lived alone in a large house near the river in Clyde Street. He was a well to do individual who dressed immaculately and thought himself to be very handsome and admired by the fairer sex; while, in fact he was rather ugly with a large, protruding nose and twisted spine.

Robert was a sad, lonely character, who, with smiles and glances in the direction of the opposite sex, would promenade up and down on the pavement outside the Tontine Building at Glasgow Cross, (an area that was known as 'The Plane Stanes'). The young ladies in question would give him a disdainful look and hurry past, then, on giving a backward glance, start to giggle at his audacity.

He was a quiet individual, who wouldn't do anyone any harm; none the less, most of the children were afraid of him and being children, cruelly mocked him and called him; 'Bob Dragon'; more often than not, they simply referred to him as 'THE DRAGON'; all except Feea, for he had a certain degree of respect for this Dandy of the Glaswegian aristocracy; in his innocence, Feea could see beyond Bob's deformity and in so doing, saw the kindness of the man himself. Where as, the other 'respected gentlemen' would shoo Feea away when ever they encountered him on the street; Bob would slip him a penny or two as he passed, for this kindness Feea would kiss Bob's hand, thanking him most profusely. Bob, with a bemused smile, would then pat the little lad's head affectionately. There was a certain element of understanding between these two eccentric characters, even though they were miles apart on the 'social ladder'. There friendship had been formed from an incident that took place the previous summer.

It was a warm day in mid-June. Some boys from The Gorbals crossed the old wooden bridge and made their way towards The Trongate, in search of trouble; they did this on occasion. There was a rivalry between the Glasgow boys and the Gorbals boys and their encounters usually ended in a stone throwing mêlée on the old wooden bridge.

But this incursion into enemy territory was merely a show of bravado on the part of this band of 'invaders' from across the river. There were eight of them, led by a real tearaway, Billy Sutton, their self appointed gang leader. Billy was a heavily built lad about fourteen years old and a reputation that was the envy of most of the young reprobates in his area. Apart from his other 'talents' which included 'head-butting' his opponents into oblivion, he had pick-pocketing down to a fine art; Billy was a nasty little piece of work.

They swaggered into the town centre pushing and shoving old ladies out of the way while at the same time, helping themselves to whatever they could steal from the frail old women's shopping baskets. They turned into the Trongate and made their way over to the King William statue at the Cross. The statue had King William of Orange sitting on his horse and holding his sceptre out in front like a sword; this was a well known meeting place in Glasgow.

Billy, with the aid of his compatriots, climbed onto the statue and sat behind the King, flapping his arms as if to mimic the actions of a bird in flight. The rest of the gang stood round the statue and laughed at the antics of their leader; much to the disgust of the passers-bye, one in particular being Bob Dreghorn; he was aghast at this lack of respect, which, to his way of thinking, was tantamount to sacrilege.

"Come down from there boy and show some respect for your betters who have gone before you!" He shouted, pointing his cane towards the offending culprit. Billy looked down at him and sneered. "Aye! Aye!!! Look at this lads, we've gote a dragon thit kin talk." The rest of the boys fell about laughing at Billy's wry humour; Bob was not amused. He changed his gaze from the upstart sitting on the statue and with a look that would have frozen the fires of hell, stared at the group of gyrating jackasses.

"What are you?...Performing monkeys? perhaps, or are you merely sheep following the bad example of your leader."

Billy jumped down from the statue and stood, menacingly in front of Bob.

"Who dae ye think yer talkin' tae?" He said, standing with his hands on his hips.

Bob ignored the question and addressed the group of ruffians.

"Why don't you all go back to where you came from and leave decent people in peace." The passers-bye were taking a wide berth to this confrontation.

Meanwhile, Feea was sitting in the doorway of the Tollbooth bell tower, watching the goings-on at the statue; he wasn't alone, for, across the street and hidden behind some clothes that were hanging on the end of a market stall, the local 'bobby', Black Jock, was also taking an interest. His partner was of a different ilk, in both build and manner. He was what you could only describe as an officious bully. He was quite short for an officer of the law. He was fat, bad tempered and his uniform could have been doing with a wash. He went by the name of Jock Matheson but the local children called him, 'Roly Poly Black Jock'; making sure that they were well out of earshot before bestowing this, less than illustrious, title on him.

Jock had no time for children; they were a constant bane on his rounds. If any of them were foolish enough to give him cheek, and they weren't quick enough, they felt the toe of his boot on their backsides as Jock believed in his own form of instant justice. Needless to say, unlike Wullie, Jock wasn't married and had no thoughts in that direction. He felt that life was troublesome enough without the added irritation of a nagging wife. Jock was in his early forties and had a handlebar moustache that joined up with his bushy sideburns.

He had drawn his truncheon and was slowly tapping it on his hand while he observed the scene on the opposite side of the street; these trouble makers were no strangers to the burly policeman. He watched as the conversation at the statue became more heated. Billy turned to one of his pals and whispered in his ear; the boy grinned and nodded. He left the group and disappeared round the back of the statue only to re-appear behind Bob; who had no idea that he was there. The boy crouched down behind him just as Billy lounged forward and, after grabbing Bob's silver tipped cane, pushed him backwards causing him to fall over the crouching boy.

That was enough for Jock, who, on witnessing the assault on Bob, dashed across the street and landed a swift kick on Billy's backside. On seeing the policeman, the others scampered in all directions. Bob lay dazed as Billy quickly picked himself up and dashed towards the Cross, clutching Bob's cane. He didn't see the foot shooting out from the doorway of the bell tower and went tumbling over as Feea grabbed the cane out of his hand. There was no time to try and retrieve it as the burly policeman was right behind him. He got up and before Jock had time to grab him, he dashed down the Saltmarket and was away back across the bridge.

Jock gave up the chase half-way down the Saltmarket and made his way back to the statue where Bob, having been helped to his feet by some passers-bye, was standing in the middle of a small crowd who had gathered and was nursing a lump on the back of his head.

"My prize cane," he said with exasperation in his voice, "the little scoundrel has run off with my silver tipped cane. It was a family heirloom and he's got away with it."

"Naw he didnae, here it's here," a voice piped up from amidst the onlookers. Feea pushed his way through the group of bystanders and handed the cane to Bob.

Bob took the cane from Feea then spoke to him with a quizzical expression on his face.

"But, why didn't you run off with the rest of them?"

"Me no like thum, they is bad," Feea said, shaking his head.

"But, how did you retrieve the cane?" Bob asked.

"Och, me tripped the bad boye up fur yae," Feea said, nodding and smiling with an impish grin on his face.

"Aye the lad's tellin' the truth a saw him dae it as nice as yae like," Jock said in his usual gruff voice, only this time there was a hint of admiration in it.

"That was very brave of you," Bob said with a broad grin on his face. He reached into his pocket and took out a shilling; he handed it to Feea.

"Take this lad, it's in appreciation for what you have done for me."

Feea looked at the coin in his hand and noticed how it glinted in the sunshine. He had never seen a coin like this before, this was silver and shiny, not like the dirty pennies and half-pennies that he was used to getting for dancing on the streets, he kissed Bob's hand, bowed before him, then kissed the coin; the smile on his face and those wide blue eyes were a sight to behold. Bob was taken aback and felt a bit embarrassed at the boy's impeccable manners, he shook Feea's hand.

"What is your name?" He asked.

"Me is Feea," came back the lilting answer.

"Well Feea it's like a breath of fresh air to meet a young man with such manners and principles, you are an example to your peers and a hope for the future. I only wish that there were more like you."

Feea had no idea what Bob was talking about, but he kept smiling and nodding his head quite erratically none the less. The little lad was in total agreement with anyone who would give him such a coin as the one that he was holding so tightly in his hand.

Bob smiled and shook his head. "Such undignified innocence," he thought to himself. From that day on he showed nothing but kindness to Feea whenever he came across him on the street.

As he left, he patted Feea on the shoulder, "You take care laddie," he said, then made his way along the Trongate. The little crowed that had gathered, dispersed, leaving Feea standing, looking at his shiny coin. Black Jock was the last to leave, but before he departed he gave Feea a piece of friendly advice.

""You look efter that coin and dinna let onybody tak' it fae yae."

Feea nodded and waved to the policeman as he crossed the street.

Word soon went round the other urchins, that Feea had a silver shilling. All the boys wanted to be his friend and help him to spend his prize, but Feea resisted their offers and held on to the coin. Meanwhile it had come to the attention of Wullie Borland, better known as 'Wullie The Weasel', a ne'r-do-well miscreant, who hung around the streets keeping an eye open for any opportunity to get some money legally or otherwise. He went over to the group of boys.

"Whit's gawn oan here," he asked, barging his way to the centre of the small group.

"It's Feea, he's gote a shullin'," one of the boys exclaimed.

"Well you lot leave him alane wae his shullin'. Go on awa ye go," he said ushering the boys away. The boys slowly wandered away muttering among themselves. The Weasel put an arm round Feea's shoulder.

"A'll mak sure they dinna get yur shullin," he said with a lear. He looked around to make sure that he wasn't being observed then looked down at Feea. "Let me see it, son."

Slowly Feea opened his hand exposing the shiny coin to the glare of The Weasel's darting, evil eyes; Wullie grinned and picked the coin out of the little lad's hand. Feea watched with a look of concern on his face as The Weasel examined it.

"Yae ken thit some o' these shullins ur no real," he said, looking down at Feea, who was staring up at him, wide eyed, open mouthed and slowly shaking his head in disbelief; he had fallen from the heights of ecstasy into the pit of doubt.

"Och wu'll soon fin' oot, a'll bounce it ofe a wa' an' see if it pings like a real shullin; aw richt," the Weasel smirked.

Feea nodded his head, his face was a picture of innocence and naivety; a fish that was about to be hooked.

"We'll dae it ofe the auld priory wa'; see, that wan ower there."

As Feea looked in the direction that The Weasel was pointing, the scoundrel switched the shilling for a halfpenny and holding it in his hand out of sight, sauntered over to the wall that surrounded the old priory. The wall was about seven feet high and had been built from sandstone blocks. It was in need of repair and had gaps along the top where some of the ancient stones had fallen down.

"Ur yae ready?" The Weasel said with an evil grin on his face.

"Aye," Feea answered, nodding his head so erratically that it was in danger of falling off.

Wullie flicked the coin hard and sent it spinning right over the top of the wall. "Och a did it too hard. Climb ower an' fetch it," he said gesturing with his thumb. No sooner had he said this than Feea was scrambling up and over the wall.

"Kin yae see it?" He called out.

"Naw, bit a'll fine' it," came a voice from the other side.

"That's richt, keep lookin'," The Weasel smirked trying to contain his laughter. Quietly he slipped away, shaking his head at how gullible the little lad had been. He disappeared down a lane and was gone, leaving Feea in his vain search for a coin that just wasn't there. After a while, Feea's voice could be heard, shouting, at the other side of the wall.

"Me's fun' a haepenny an a dod a' string." When there was no answer he called again. "Kin yae hear me, kin yae hear me mister?"

Then two dirty hands appeared at the top of the wall followed by Feea's head. "A fun a haep...enny..." Feea's words faded away as his eyes scanned the deserted street. He wondered where the man that had been so helpful had gone. He shrugged his shoulders and then climbed back down and continued his search. He searched for the rest of the day and returned every day for a week raking through the long grass with his hands. He kept it a secret, just in case some of the other boys learned about his misfortune, and found the shilling for themselves. This had been the first but not the last time that Feea and The Weasel would cross paths.

# JAMIE

It was a warm Saturday afternoon in mid-July.

Feea was sitting on a wooden box looking up at the sky and wondering where the scattered puffs of white cloud were going as they made their meandering way across the heavens. While pondering this, 'tumultuous' problem, he heard the sound of singing coming from the Trongate. Now this was more to his understanding and, on climbing down from the box, made his way to the sweet sound of the music. When he turned into the street, he saw a group of wandering minstrels performing over at the Tollbooth. They were singing ' Gypsy Laddie', one of Feea's favourite songs. The passers-by weren't paying much attention to the singers and the hat lay empty on the ground. Feea went over and started to dance in front of the merry band, almost at once people stopped and watched this little bare footed boy prancing and gyrating to the music. Soon a crowd had gathered and were cheering and applauding every pirouette and jump. When the song was finished .the pavement rang to the sound of coins as the crowd showed their appreciation. Feea gathered the coins and put them in the hat in front of the singers. The one called Jamie put his guitar down and went over to speak to the little lad;

"Whit's yer name laddie?" He asked, at the same time casting a glance into the hat.

"Me is Feea," the little boy answered as he stood with feet apart and his hands on his hips.

"Weel, Feea yer a fine dancer. Will ye dance again fur us?" The man asked with a smile.

"Och aye, me will dance fur ye, me likes tae dance a' richt." He said, flicking his hair out of his eyes.

"Whit's yer favourite song?" the man enquired.

"Me like Kullykanky the bestest." Feea answered excitedly. Jamie went back over to the others and, picking up his guitar, turned to them and asked with a grin;

"Will we play Killiecrankie fur Feea, lads?"

They answered in unison. "Och aye a think we kin manage that a' richt," and started to play. The crowd grew larger as Feea danced, there were cheers and gasps as he leapt and gyrated.

The gathering of such a large crowd drew the attention of two unsavoury characters standing on the far corner, namely, Wullie 'The Weasel and Malky Monachan, his partner in crime.

The men glanced at each other, then, with a sly grin; made their way over to the crowd, where there would be good pickings for agile fingers such as the Weasel's. They worked as a team; Malky did the jostling while The Weasel did the picking.

When they got over to the crowd, Wullie picked out a likely victim while Malky positioned himself at his side. On this occasion, their unknowing benefactor was a tall business like gentleman. Malky bumped into him and before the man had time to regain his balance; his wallet was gone and was making its way down the Saltmarket in The Weasel's grubby inside pocket. Malky left and followed his compatriot down the street. Feea had just finished dancing when a commotion broke out. There was cry of 'PICKPOCKET', as the businessman accused all and sundry that were around him. Bert the cooper didn't take too kindly to being prodded in the ribs by the irate gentleman and swiftly planted a hefty blow on his chin; it was every man for himself after that. Fists were flying and boots were swinging as the gathering of law-abiding citizens turned into a fracas. Rab the rat catcher had his first wash for months when someone dumped him into the horse trough, causing the horse that was drinking from it to panic and make off along the Trongate with boxes and barrels flying off the cart in all directions. Right in the middle of the melee an' old 'dowager duchess' was prodding her walking cane into the stomach of a timid little man and accusing him of every despicable act in the book. The poor man in turn was trying to defend himself and denying every vile accusation while at the same time, trying to detach a little mongrel that had sunk its teeth into his ankle and was holding on like grim death. Muldoon the innkeeper held one man by the throat while he dug his elbow into the ribs of another would be 'contender'. Meanwhile, Feea and the group of merry minstrels had quietly disappeared into the High Street leaving 'The Battle of the Tron' to sort itself out.

They sat down on a grassy knoll opposite the College while Jamie counted the array of coins that were in the hat. Feea sat cross-legged in front of the men and was more interested in a ladybird that was making its way through the blades of grass. To his simple mind, this was a little explorer lost in the jungle of some far off land. He placed his hand in front of the insect and giggled as it crawled over his fingers before spreading its wings and flying off to a more exotic location in the grounds of the Old College.

" We'll be eating to-day", Jamie announced when he had finished counting the coins, " an' its all due tae this wee laddie," he said pointing to Feea, who was still watching the progress of the ladybird as it flew over the railings and disappeared into the rhododendron bushes at the side of the college gatehouse. The men got up and were about to walk away when Jamie turned to Feea, who was still sitting on the grass,

"Weel, laddie, whit are you waiting fur; are ye no hungry?"

"Och aye, me is awfae hungry," Feea said with his eyes wide in anticipation.

"Weel come alang wae us an' we'll gang doon tae the tavern fur some ham houghs." Feea jumped to his feet and followed the men back down the High Street, skipping and dancing as he went. When they passed the cross, the mêlée' had quietened down to a 'minor riot', the two police officers had arrived and were in the thick of it. Wullie Balornock was trying to separate two women who were intent on pulling each other's hair out by the roots, while Black Jock was running about, bonking all and sundry with his cudgel. Jamie and the group gave the mêlée a wide berth and went down the Saltmarket where they entered the tavern. They sat down at a table near the door. The barmaid came over and gave it a wipe.

"What can I get for you gentlemen?" She asked, straightening the front of her apron. This was Jean Muldoon, the proprietor's daughter.

"Ham haughs an' ale a' roon," Jamie announced banging a pile of coins on the table and giving his hands a rub. Jean went through into the kitchen as the men settled down at the table with Feea sitting at the end nearest the door. Just then, Paddy Muldoon came in rubbing his hands as if he were washing them.

"That was a fine scrap to be sure," he said in a broad Irish accent.

"Sure, it gives a man a fair tirst," he added as he made his way behind the bar. When he had poured himself a drink and swallowed it down, he looked over at the group sitting near the door;

"Are ye beein' served gentlemen?" he asked, filling his glass again.

"Aye, the young lady's takin' good care of us," Jamie answered.

"Are ye not the lads that were playin' such fine music at the Cross when the stramash broke out, an' is that not the wee lad that wis dancin' like a leprechaun round a toadstool?"

"Aye that's wis us aw richt an' this is Feea, the best wee dancer in the toon." Jamie answered, making a gesture in Feea's direction. The little lad smiled shyly then turned his head and looked out the door. He noticed Scruff sniffing about in the lane opposite. He watched the little dog for a few minutes, then, after running from one side to the other it, disappeared up the lane; probably in pursuit of some mangy old tomcat. Feea turned his attention to a flea that had decided to have lunch on his bum. After having a good claw at it, he turned back to the others and sat with his legs crossed, listening to the conversation.

"Would ye be knowin' any songs from the old country?" Paddy asked, using a rag to wipe some sweat from his brow.

"Aye we dae, wid ye like tae hear wan?" Jamie answered.

"Sure now, I'd be obliged," Paddy said as the men got their instruments ready. He came round from behind the bar and sat on the edge of a table as Jamie started to sing a sad song from County Donegal. When he had finished, Paddy took the rag that he had used to wipe the sweat from his brow and used it to wipe a tear from his eye. "Sure, ye sang it so beautifully that I could almost smell the grass outside me dear departed mother's cottage; God bless her." Paddy made the Sign of the Cross, then, after wiping his eyes again, blew his nose on the rag.

"Yer a fine group of musicians, to be sure an' it gladdens me heart that ye have come into me own humble establishment. Where is it that yer stayin'?"

"We're camped oot b' the village o' Grahamstoon", Jamie said, gesturing over his shoulder with his thumb.

"Oh, Grahamstown would it be, 'tis lovely there with the hills risin' above it, ye know, where they herd the cattle before they bring them down into the town on their way to the market, Oi t'ink they call it Cowcuddence, or somt'n loik tat. Sure, Mrs Muldoon and me-self go there for a walk after church; when the weather's foin tat is. It's noice to see the cattle grazing in the fields near the woods; it's so peaceful after the hustle and bustle of the town. How long will you be staying there?"

"Och, we'll be there fur a wee while," Jamie answered. "It's a gid camp-site an' the man who owns the sawmill said that he micht hae some work fur us noo an' then; so in between times we kin go roon the villages earnin' a crust, wae daein' whit we dae best."

"Aye singin', drinkin an' wenchin," one of the others piped up. "Aye, bit they dinna need tae be in that order," Jamie added. They all burst out laughing and nodded there agreement. Paddy smiled. "Sure now, that's a job that was made in heaven," he said with just the slightest hint of envy in his voice. Jean came in from the kitchen carrying a huge tray with plates of steaming meat on them. She put it down on the table and the men helped themselves to a plate each; Jamie put one in front of Feea, whose eyes widened at the sight of the banquet before him; the little lad didn't stand on, ceremony and delved straight in with both hands. Noticing Feea's uncouth table manners, Jamie nudged his friend sitting beside him and gestured towards the scene at the end of the table. The man smiled, "That's it son, you gie it lalldy," he said with a chuckle in his voice; the rest of the men giggled at Feea's onslaught on the ham haugh.

When they had finished their meal, Feea took a bone from his plate and left. He made his way up the lane to see where Scruff had gone. He went through a close and into the backcourt. At the far end of the backcourt some boys were kneeling in a circle; Feea recognised one of them and called over.

"Boaby, me is lookin' fur Scruff, a've gote a bone fur him. Did ye see where he went? Ah seen him runnin' up the lane, bit a dinna ken whaur he is noo."

"Naw ah hivnae seen him efter that, he's maybe doon at the Fleshers' Haugh." Bobby replied and then turned back to the other boys who were engrossed in a game of shove-happeny.

Feea left and headed towards the Fleshers' Haugh which was situated beside the Green and was the oldest abattoir in Glasgow; every stray dog in the town seemed to find its way there in search of titbits at one time or another. The men who worked there seemed to spend a lot of time chasing them away.

Feea wandered down the Saltmarket, followed by a little pack of dogs who had got a sniff of the ham bone that he was carrying. The boldest of the pack were jumping up to try and get to the prize but Feea shoved them away telling them that it was for Scruff; as if they knew what he was saying. The little lad was like 'The Pied Piper' leading the rats out of town. While he was shooing the other dogs away, a scraggy mongrel jumped up and sunk its teeth into the ham bone, wrenching it right out of Feea's hand. Before the little lad had time to retrieve it, the dog was off up an alley with Feea in hot pursuit; needless to say, Scruff never did get that bone.

# BLIND ALICK

It was a warm Sunday evening. The streets were quiet, except for the lonely strains of a violin. Blind Alick was standing on a corner serenading to anyone that would care to listen but mostly it was for his own pleasure as music was his greatest love. He had been blind from childhood and being so, his hearing had become very acute. This led to his ability for not only hearing the music but to actually feel and experience the emotion of the melody. Although he was only a beggar on the streets, he was in a class of his own. Alick was an undeniable virtuoso in his own right. His long hair gave him the appearance of a maestro, and, humble though he was, it was no illusion. He was a kindly man who kept to himself and whose talent was admired and appreciated by his contemporaries. The sweet tones from his violin reached the ears of Feea who was sitting in a backclose at the bottom of a street nearby. The hypnotic melody seemed to drift through the closes and fill the rectangular courtyard behind the tenement buildings. He listened to the music as he watched two rats playing at the side of an upturned crate near the wall. He watched them scurry away as the sound of footsteps approached the close entrance. Two men stopped at the front of the close and continued the discussion they were having. Feea sat in the darkness and listened; the topic was Blind Alick.

"It'll be nae bother, the blin' fiddler wullnae see us cumin', an' thur's naebody aboot onywie. Awe you need tae dae is grab his erms while a pit the bag ower his heed an' hod his mooth. Then wull drag him intae a backclose an' smother him. Jist think, big yin, wu'll get pied fur him up at the College an' wu'll get a shullin' or twa fur his fiddle as weel. Och aye, wu'll be boozin' the nicht that's fur sure." Feea strained his eyes to see if he could make out who was speaking, but all he could see was two shapes, one large and one small, the smaller of the two seemed to be doing all the talking. "Noo remember, grab his erms an' a'll bag 'im."

When Feea realised what was about to take place, he quietly slipped away and ran across the backcourt and through a close. He emerged near the corner of the street where Blind Alick was playing. Without stopping, he ran up to the blind musician, grabbed his arm and stopped him from playing.

"Whit's awe this? Who's ther'? The man exclaimed, having been taken by surprise.

"It me, fiddle man, it me Feea. Bad mannies is cumin' tae hurt yae. Come oan, me wull help yae tae get awa." He took the man's hand and almost dragged him along the street. Alick tried to match Feea's pace but the best he could do was a quick, hesitant shuffle. They turned into an alley just as the two, would be assailants, arrived on the street.

"Ther' he goes, Weasel, he's gawn doon the Back Wynd, the larger man shouted.

"Shut up, ah see'im, an stoap shoutin' ma name ya dope," the other man said with exasperation in his voice.

The alley was lined with crates and boxes piled high on either side. Feea and Alick were about halfway down the alley when they heard the crunching footsteps of their pursuers at the top. Feea let go of the man's hand;

"Keep gaw'n fiddle man, a'll stoap them," the boy shouted as he ran over to the piles of crates. The old man hurried as best he could while Feea grabbed at the bottom crate. He put his foot against the wall and pulled as hard as he could until it began to move. The whole pile began to sway as he kept pulling and jerking at the crate, then, with a loud creak followed by a crash, the crates and boxes crashed down across the alley. The impact on the opposite pile caused them to sway and fall hitting another pile. Feea ran for his life as pile after pile came crashing down, completely blocking the alley. A tirade of cursing and swearing came from the other side of the mound of crates.

"Come on we'll go roon the other wei an' catch thum at the boatum o' the street," the small man said angrily. The men ran back up the alley and turned into the street that they had come from.

Meanwhile Feea and Alick had made their way out of the alley and had crossed over to the street that ran along the side of McGurk's stable. Feea led Alick over to the secret entrance to the stable. He pulled the loose board back and tugged at Alick's swallow tailed-coat as he whispered in his ear.

"Coorie doon an' we'll hide in ma secrit den".

The fiddler crouched down and Feea pushed him to the opening. The old man shakily felt his way and, with the little boy's help, squeezed through followed by Feea, who slid the wooden plank back into position.

"Shush!" Feea whispered as they stood in the dark. They listened in the inky blackness as the sound of crunching footsteps approached and held their breath when they stopped right outside the secret entrance. They heard a man speak, he sounded out of breath.

"Where did they go? Ah saw thum come doon this wie. See if thu've gawn up that lane?" There was the sound of footsteps fading away then they came back and another voice spoke,

"Naw thur no' up ther, maybe thuv gawn tae the Green?"

"Och it disnae maiter noo, thu've gote away, so we better jist furget awe aboot grabbin' the fiddler, seein' thit you've let him ken ma name. He's bound tae tell his cronies, so if onythin happened tae him then we'd be the first wans thit they'd come lookin fur."

Just at that moment, there was a screech as Alick's violin rubbed against the side of a stall.

"Whit's that, did yae hear that noays' it sounded like a fiddle."

The big man had no sooner said that, than a cat went tearing across the street followed by Scruff in hot pursuit.

"A Fiddle? Ya edjit! That's whit ye heard, it's a cat," the Weasel remarked in utter frustration as he pointed in the direction of the two animals running into a close.

"Noo, come oan an' wu'll see if we kin find anither patient fur the doactur, if no', then we kin aye check oot the Ramshorn later oan."

Alick breathed a sigh as he listened to their footsteps fading away.

There was an air of relief in Alick's voice as he sunk to the ground and sat with Feea in the darkness. He let out a long drawn out sigh.

"Och laddie, that wis close. Ah thoacht we were done fur when ma fiddle scraped agin' the wa'."

"Me thoat yae wis gonnae play a jig fur the hoarses," Feea retorted in all innocence. Alick and Feea started to giggle at the very thought of it. They waited for a while; then made their way back through the opening and out into the street. Feea walked with Alick until they got to his house. The fiddler invited the boy inside but Feea declined the invitation saying that he was going to look for Scruff. Before leaving, he thanked Alick for his hospitality. Alick in turn, thanked Feea for his kindness and concern and gave him a hug saying that he would never forget that night. Feea kissed his hand and ran off into the night.

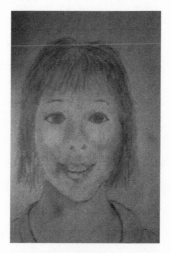

**CURDIE**

It was a winter morning four days before Christmas. A bitterly cold wind swept across a thick blanket of snow that was covering Glasgow Green. Feea and Scruff made their way through the crisp snowfield towards the Saltmarket, when Scruff disappeared into the bushes and started barking excitedly. Feea stopped and, on looking back, called out for the little dog to come out from the bushes, but it just kept on barking. Feea, huffily, made his way back to the bushes where Scruff was barking. "Scruff, here! Scruff, it too cauld tae play." The little dog ignored him and continued. Feea made his way into the bushes, getting covered in falling snow with every step. He saw Scruff parading backwards and forwards, near what looked like a bundle of rags lying on the ground, he was very agitated. Feea went over and looked down to see a young boy apparently asleep and covered in snow, his skin was blue with the cold. Feea tried to waken him but he didn't stir. He bent down and with great effort lifted him into his arms and made his way out of the bushes. He ploughed his way through the deep snow, past the Nelson Monument and on to the Saltmarket with Scruff yelping at his heels. He was completely exhausted as he laid the boy down outside the tavern.

Just then, Wullie Balornock appeared. He was on his way home after finishing his night patrol. On noticing Feea huddled over the boy, he went over to see what he was doing.

"Whit dae we hiv here?" He inquired, with a quizzical expression on his face. Feea looked up at the tall policeman;

"Boye no wake, him wiz layin' in the bushes, he no movin' ata."

The policeman crouched down and took a close look at the unconscious boy.

"We'll hiv tae get him wa'rm as soon as we kin," he said, lifting the little boy into his arms. He carried the boy up the Saltmarket, closely followed by Feea and Scruff.

They turned into a street and went up to a house. Wullie asked Feea to knock on the door, which he did. The door opened and a woman with a grey shawl wrapped round her shoulders stood looking at Wullie. "Whit's happened?" She asked looking down at the little boy in her husband's arms. Feea stepped back apprehensively and stood at the side.

"The bairn's near frozen tae death", Wullie said as he made his way into the house. Feea and Scruff waited outside as the woman followed her husband indoors. She got some blankets and put them down in front of the hearth. Wullie laid the boy on them and covered him while his wife put some more coal on the fire. Wullie turned to her;

"Tell wee Feea tae come inside oot the caul', an' shut the ootside door". Mrs Balornock went to the door but Feea and Scruff had gone. Feea didn't like women in houses. Separately he didn't mind but together they made him feel threatened. Mrs Balornock closed the door and returned to the living room.

"Where's Feea?" Wullie asked, seeing his wife come back alone.

"He must've ran aff, thur wis nae sign o' him, ur his wee dug," she answered, Wullie just shook his head.

"Well we better see tae this wee mite. See if ye kin heat up some o' that broth thit ye made last nicht an' we'll try 'n get him tae tak some." Mrs Balornock moved a black pot onto the range while Wullie rubbed the little boy's arms and legs in an attempt to get his circulation going again.

It was almost an hour before the little boy started to show signs of life. He slowly opened his eyes and looked around. When he saw Wullie's uniform, he drew back. There was fear in his eyes as he gazed at the policeman.

"Dinna tak me back there mister, gonnae no'?" he begged.

"A'm no' takin' yae onywhere son, yer jist gonnae lie ther 'til ye feel a bit better," Wullie assured him.

Mrs Balornock poured some broth into a bowl. She took a spoonful and after blowing on it, offered it to the boy.

"Come on now tak some o' this, it will warm you up," she said putting the spoon to the boy's lips. He started to gulp it down. It was the first food that he had eaten in four days.

"No' sae fast, there's mer in the pot for ye," she said with a smile.

The boy smiled back and sipped the soup.

It transpired that he had run away from a workhouse in Ayrshire, where he had been badly treated; the bruises on his back bore witness to that. His name was Hamish MacCurdie, he was twelve years old and an orphan.

Wullie told him how Feea had found him on the Green and how, if it hadn't been for Feea carrying him into town, he would, surely, have died out there in the bitter cold.

"Who is Feea?" the boy asked; Wullie smiled.

"He's a wee lad like yersel'. He lives oan the streets an' och he's a good boye an' disna gie us onae bother. He tends tae bide in a wee world o' his ain, bit ye'll like him; everybody likes wee Feea, he's a funny wee lad who widna dae herm tae naebody."

A few days later, when he had completely recovered, the boy left and went in search of Feea. Wullie had told him that Feea could usually be found either at Glasgow Cross or on the Green. He went to the Green first but it was deserted, except for two boys who were building a snowman at the side of the Monument.

Plowing through the deep snow, he went over and spoke to them.

"Kin yae tell me where a kin fun the boye caud Feea?" he asked.

One of the boys looked up and pointed to-wards the town.

"Aye, he's at the Cross, ye'll see him there, he's werrin a wee blue jaiket." After imparting this piece of information, the boy continued with the work at hand, namely rolling a ball of snow that would make the snowman's head. Hamish left and made his way back into the town. When he got to the Cross, he started looking for a boy in a blue jacket. As his eyes scanned the area, they settled on a lonely figure huddled at the side of the King William statue. He went over and stood in front of the chitterling figure. "Ur you the boye caud Feea,"

"Aye, F...F...Feea is me," Feea answered through chittering teeth. He was rubbing his arm to try and get some warmth back into it as the jacket he was wearing had seen better days. It only had one sleeve and the other one was hanging by a thread. He looked at Hamish for a minute then smiled.

"Ur you the boye thit a fun oan the Green? Ur yae awe richt noo?" He asked with genuine concern in his voice.

"Och a'm awe richt thanks tae you," Hamish answered. "Ma name is Hamish, Hamish MacCurdie," he added holding his hand out in greeting. Feea stood for a moment, not knowing how to react. Hamish grabbed his hand and shook it warmly. Feea was a bit startled then a broad grin came over his face.

"Curdie, me gets curdies fur dancin' sometimes, it's a funny name, bit me likes it;" and that was the name that Feea called Hamish from that day on. They became the best of friends and although Feea was a loner, he would look out for Curdie so that they could play together. They grew very close, almost like brothers and God help the boy who would ever say anything against Feea or try to ridicule him in Curdie's company.

# PANIC AT THE CROSS

It was a warm Saturday morning in mid-July. The Trongate was bustling with people scurrying here and there, as they went about their business. There were many carts and carriages on the street and in the midst of the hubbub could be heard shouting as the various merchants called out their wares.

The water seller was doing a roaring trade as the people queued up to quench their thirst. There was the sound of screeching and grinding as the knife sharpener plied his trade near the corner of Candleriggs Street.

Feea was watching the thronging crowds as he sat by the side of King William's statue, which was in the middle of the street oposite the Tontine Tea Room. Scruff lay sleeping at his feet, oblivious to all that was taking place around him. Maggie the flower seller had made her pitch with a profusion of colourful blooms at the end of the statue that faced along the Trongate. She called to the crowd while holding a bunch of brightly coloured flowers in her hand and as soon as they were sold, they would be replaced with another. Across the street Andy McGurk was delivering some barrels of ale to the tavern on the corner while, just up the High Street, Wee Geordie Knox, the fruit seller, was serving some customers from an over-laden barrow that he had propped against a wall. Meanwhile, big Daphne Etherston was making her way down the High Street, all twenty-four, seething, stone of her, and she looked like someone was about to be on the receiving end of her wrath. From about ten yards away she started shouting; "Knox, ya thievin' wee scoundrel, ah wa'nt a word wae yae!" Wee Geordie turned, apprehensively, in her direction; "Oh, it's you Mrs Etherton. Whit kin a dae fur yae? It's a nice day isn't it?" he grovelled with a weak smile that fooled no one, especially Daphne Etherton. Daphne stared right into his face; "A nice day is it? Don't gie me ony aye yur snash ur a'll belt yer lug fur yae; ya wee rat! Whit dae yae caw these when they're at hame?" She tipped her basket over, emptying, what appeared to be rotten potatoes, onto the ground.

"Dae yae think yae kin tak advantage o' ma wee lassie, is that yer gemme? Ya wee skunner." (Daphne's 'wee lassie' was eleven years old and weighed fourteen stone).

"Thur...thur no mine she must hae gote thum sumwher' else," the little man stammered. Maggie grabbed him by the throat;

"Somewher' else? Are ye cau'n ma wee lassie a liar noo? Is that it? Yer cau'n ma wee Primrose a liar." Daphne went to punch Wee Geordie but he wriggled clear, causing the big woman to stumble and go careering into the barrow. The force of the impact dislodged it from the wall and sent it rolling down the High Street towards the Cross. Apples, pears and all manner of vegetables were cascading from the barrow as it gained speed on its unstoppable journey, followed by the irate Geordie waving his arms in the air and screaming for someone to stop it. People were running in all directions in an attempt to get out of its way.

The barrow went flying through the Cross and crashed into McGurk's cart, throwing the carter to the ground and causing the horse to take off in a panic. Both horse and cart went careering towards a group of people in the centre of the street. They ran out of its way, that is, all except a young woman called Margaret Roxburgh, who was crossing the street to meet her fiancé who was waiting for her on the other side. On seeing the terrified horse approach, she screamed and fainted, right in its path.

At that moment, Feea sprang to his feet and ran out into the path of the oncoming horse.

"Bella!!!...Bella!!!...It me, Feea!" He called out, waving his arms in the air. The old horse reared up when it recognized the voice of the person who brought it little treats of carrots and other goodies. It skidded to a halt on the smooth cobblestones just in front of Feea and the unconscious young woman. Feea went over and patted its neck as it snorted and shook its head.

A small crowd gathered and were patting Feea on the back and congratulating him for his bravery, while another group including Margaret's fiancé, William

Caldwell, had gathered round her and were helping her to her feet.

Maggie the flower seller's attention was drawn to a little girl crying, hysterically, at the side of her pitch. In all the confusion, she had become separated from her mother. Maggie went over and consoled her until her mother appeared in an irate condition a few moments later. Meanwhile, Andy McGurk had managed to extricate himself from the pile of boxes and straw that he had landed in and was over adding his congratulations to the 'little hero'. Feea, not being used to all the attention that he was being given, got a bit panicky. He ducked under the cart, came out at the other side and ran down a side street closely followed by Scruff, who was yelping his head off and thinking that it was all a game.

Meanwhile, Margaret recovered and was being comforted by her fiancé.

"Where did the boy go," William asked, looking around.

"What boy?" Margaret replied somewhat mystified.

"The little boy who saved you're life." William answered, looking over at the cart.

"The little boy who saved my life?... I don't understand," Margaret said with a surprised look on her face.

"When you fainted, a little boy ran out in front of the horse and cart, and, somehow, stopped them. I've never seen such bravery and it must not go unrewarded," William explained. He turned to a man standing with his wife; "Did you see where the little lad went?"

"Aye, he ran doon the Saltmarket towards the Green wae his wee dug," the man answered.

"You wouldn't know the little lad's name by any chance? William enquired.

"Och aye, its Feea, wee Feea, he dances fur pennies near the Tollbooth. He's aye ther'near every day," the man answered

"Where does he stay," William asked.

"Och, he disnae stiye onywhere, he sleeps in back closes or auld stables, onywhere he kin fine' that he kin keep wa'rm in." With that, the man took his wife's arm and left.

"Are you feeling all right now? William asked his fiancé.

"Yes I'm fine," she said, knocking some dust off her long skirt.

"Well, I'll take you home and then I'll go and see if I can find this Feea, I'd like to thank him personally for what he did. It's only a week until our wedding and I nearly lost you" He gave her a hug and then they made their way to William's coach that was standing across the street. They climbed on board and after giving instructions to the driver, they set off to Margaret's home in Charlotte Street. After being assured that she was all right, he left, climbed back onto the coach and made his way towards Glasgow Green. The Green lay at the bottom of the Saltmarket and was a favourite play area for the children of that locale. When he arrived, he started looking for the lad but couldn't see him anywhere. He noticed some boys playing near the Nelson Monument. He left the coach and went over to speak to them.

"Have you seen a lad called Feea about?" One of the boys turned and pointed.

"Aye he's ower ther' lying doon near the bushes." William thanked him and went in the direction that the boy had been pointing.

Feea was lying back, dozing in the warm sunshine; Scruff was lying at his feet as William approached. The little dog looked up, then jumped to its feet and gave a warning 'yelp' as he got closer.

Feea stirred and turned his head in the direction of the approaching footsteps.

"Hello, is your name Feea?" William asked, while keeping an eye on Scruff, who was doing likewise. Feea sat up and rubbed his eyes.

"Aye, me is Feea," he answered, "an' him is Scruff," he said, pointing to the little dog at his feet.

"I'm pleased to meet you Feea. My name is William Caldwell" William said, holding out his hand in greeting. Feea got up and, with a little bow, kissed the back of William's hand. William smiled, having been taken aback by the little boy's unexpected gesture.

"May I sit beside you?" he asked. Feea nodded his head and swept some dead leaves away with his hand. William sat down and turned to him.

"That was a very brave thing that you did up at the Cross. You know that you could well have saved the life of someone very dear to me."

"Bella no wa'nt tae hurt naebody, Bella wis feert," Feea blurted out in defence of the old horse.

"I understand, Feea, but it's not the horse that I want to talk about; it's you." William had taken an instant liking to the little lad and wanted to show his appreciation for what he had done.

"Where do you stay, Feea?"

"Me stiye here in Glesca," the little boy answered in all innocence.

"Yes, but I mean, where do you sleep?"

"Och, me seep in loats a' places, aw ower the toon," he said, pointing towards the town. William nodded in quiet understanding.

"Where are your mother and father?" William noticed the pained look on the little boy's face and wished that he hadn't asked that question. Feea changed the subject;

" Is the lady aw richt noo? Ah didna get time tae help her when aw the people came aroon me, a' gote feert an me 'n Scruff ran awa."

William put his hand on Feea's shoulder;

"She's fine, thanks to your brave actions. You're a good lad and I would like to do something for you; if you'll let me that is. I believe that you are rather fond of horses, is that right?"

"Och aye me gets oan weel wae aw the hoarses in the toon," Feea said.

"Well I am getting married next Saturday and then I'll be leaving for a short holiday, but when I get back I'll be returning to my Father's estate; there are lots of horses in the stables. How would you like to come and see them? You could have a little holiday and see the other animals that are there as well; would you like that?"

"Och aye, an' Scruff, kin he come tae?" Feea said excitedly.

"He certainly can," William assured him. Feea got up and started to jump up and down shouting, "Goody-goody," and hugging his benefactor as he did so. Scruff started jumping up and down and yelping at his side. William smiled at the antics of the two of them.

He extricated himself from Feea's over-zealous hugging and tried to calm him down. "Take it easy or you'll do yourself an injury," he said laughing. "Well that's settled then; where will you be on Saturday," William asked with a quizzical look on his face.

Feea looked up at him and gave his shoulders a little shrug.

"Me wull be up at the Cross listenin' tae the singers." He answered.

"Good, make sure that you're there and I'll have a little surprise for you," William said, gesturing with his finger. Feea didn't answer but quickly nodded his head to show that he understood.

The tall business man bid Feea farewell and went back over to his coach. As the coachman held the door open for him, William whispered something in his ear while pointing towards Feea.

William's family were in shipping and he was down from his Father's estate at Craigavon to check that every thing was in order before one of their ships set sail for a trip to Europe. While he was in town he had intended to take the opportunity to meet his fiancé, do some shopping and make final plans for their wedding, but as always happens, fate stepped in with a few plans of its own. William got into the coach and gave Feea a wave as it moved off. Feea waved back excitedly as Scruff took of in pursuit, only to turn back as the coach left the Green.

# A CELEBRATION

It was Saturday just before noon and the warm sunshine had brought out a
veritable throng of shoppers. Feea was sitting at the edge of the paved section
of the street and looking around for the surprise that William had promised; as if
he expected it to fall from the sky; he wondered why there were no musicians
about. While he was looking up at the building across the street, William's
coach drew up. The driver climbed down and held the door open; he addressed
Feea.

"Come on laddie, my master has sent me to collect you."

Feea looked mystified.

"It's the gentleman you met on the Green the other day," he continued.

"Och yae mean Mr Coddell," Feea said with eyes wide in anticipation.

The coachman smiled. "Yes that's right; he has a surprise for you, so climb on
board."

Feea climbed into the coach and sat down on the seat by the window; he was
beaming as the coachman secured the door and climbed back into his seat. Feea
sat with a look of utter amazement on his face; he had never been in anything
like this before and felt like The King of the Castle, as he looked out at the
passers-bye.

 The coach left the Cross and turned up High Street where it stopped outside a
tailors shop. The coachman climbed down and opened the coach door.

"Come on Feea, were going to get you some clothes," the coachman said as he
helped Feea out of the coach. They went into the tailors. After about half an
hour, they emerged with Feea wearing a new jacket and trousers not to mention
a white shirt and brown cap and to top it all, he was wearing a pair of shiny, new
shoes that the tailor had sent out for. The little lad was hobbling, as he wasn't
used to wearing shoes. The coachman helped him back into the coach. Then

with the door secured, the coachman climbed back up into his seat and they were off again.

The celebration was in full swing when the coach pulled into the drive of the Grand mansion house. The guests were milling around on the lawn and everyone seemed to have a glass of wine in there hand. Feea looked out of the coach window in awe at the row of tables, where the guests were helping themselves to all manner of food and tit-bits. There was chicken, turkey, grouse, lamb chops, pork chops, venison, salmon, trout, and on one table there was every type of fruit from cherries to mangos, produce from the four corners of the earth. There were little groups scattered about deep in conversation. A rather large portly gentleman was standing in a group near a tall oak tree and every now and then he would burst out into guffaws of laughter and thump his cane on the ground. When the coach came to a halt William came running over and opened the coach door.

"Ah, Feea my boy, welcome to my wedding celebration. I hardly recognised you in your new clothes; you look very smart indeed. Come and meet my guests." He helped Feea out of the coach, and taking him by the hand, led him over to the group of gentlemen standing near the oak tree. He addressed the small group.

"This is Feea, the bravest little lad in Glasgow," he announced proudly. The men gathered round Feea, patting him on the back and shaking his hand. The portly gentleman patted Feea's head. He spoke with an English accent.

"We've heard all about you young Feea, well done lad, damn good show, you should get a medal for your bravery, damn good show." The others piped in with a chorus of "Here! Here!" and started patting him on the back again. Feea didn't know where to look, he had never been shown this much attention before, he looked embarrassed and stared down at the ground. The little group fell silent for a moment, then, right out of the blue came a sound like a foghorn as the large man expelled some wind; it was a real trouser ripper. Feea looked up in amazement and then burst out laughing; the others followed his lead, now it was the turn of the portly man to look a little embarrassed. This had been a weakness all his life and with a name like Bartholomew Carter and his particular weakness, he didn't have a very happy childhood, especially at school where he went by the nicknames of 'Bart the Fart' or 'Carter the Farter'; children tended to be rather cruel to their tubby classmates at boarding school and that applies as much to today's children as it did then; something's don't change.

A few of the elegantly dressed ladies that were standing near bye, turned and looked down their noses with a look of utter disgust and with them being downwind of the expulsion, flicked open their fans in an effort to waft away the foul smell that followed.

"Ooh! It stinky," Feea exclaimed, while holding his nose and giggling. "That wis a good wan," he added with a note of admiration in his voice; this caused the big man to giggle as well and in so doing inadvertently let out a lesser encore which made the men burst out in guffaws of laughter again.

When they had composed themselves, William took Feea's hand.

"Come on lad and we'll see if we can find you something to eat. I'll see you later gentlemen," he called out as he made his way to the tables of food. "Bye, Feea ," the men called out and gave a wave. Feea turned and waved back, almost falling over; his shoes were going to take some getting used to. When they reached the tables Feea's eyes grew wider as he observed the array of food; this was more than he had ever seen in his life. He stood in front of the banquet with mouth gaping. William released Feea's hand.

"Well, lad, what are you waiting for? Help yourself." The words were no sooner out of his mouth when Feea delved in with both hands, grabbing pieces of roast chicken, turkey, pork and anything that he could reach and stuffing as much as he could into his mouth while, at the same time, filling his pockets and packing what he could under his jacket; it was a frenzy but only Feea was taking part.. William stood back with a look of amazement on his face. The scene hadn't gone un-noticed by one of the guests, namely an elderly lady standing at the far end of the table. She was about to, daintily, pick up a small piece of chicken when she froze in her tracks; the look on her face was a mixture of shock and disbelief.

With an indignant look, she uttered, "Huh, indeed! Then, turned on her heels, and, abandoning the piece of chicken, quickly walked away muttering to herself.

William, gently, put his hand on Feea's wrist, just as he was about to grab another piece of chicken.

"Hold on lad, you don't have to do that; there's plenty more; more than you could possibly eat."

"Bit me wan'ts some fur Scruff as weel," Feea spluttered; his cheeks were bulging with the amount of food that he had stuffed in his mouth.

William smiled.

"I'll see to it that you have some food to take away with you; so, while no one is looking, put the food that you don't need just now, back on the table."

Reluctantly Feea did as William said, but, none the less, he kept a chicken leg in each of his pockets; just in case the food did run out. Just then, William heard his name being called.

"You eat as much as you want and I'll see you in a few moments. I have to go and speak to some of my guests, so have a good time and I'll see you when I return."

Feea who had his mouth full again, could only nod his agreement. William left and Feea returned to the task in hand, namely to eat as much as he could.

When he had eaten all that he could eat, Feea wandered off to explore the grounds of the great house. He sat down on the grass and took his shoes and socks off. He lay back with his arms for support as he wiggled his toes. His attention was drawn to a group of children playing over bye the garden wall. There were two boys and two girls; they were all about the same age as Feea. The boys were showing off by doing handstands against the wall while the girls cheered them on. The taller of the two had no trouble hoisting his body up to the full stretch of his arms, while his less athletic friend tended to struggled. They soon got bored with this, and as the girls giggled the boys started to do cartwheels on the grass. The smaller lad was better built for this and managed to do two. His friend pushed him aside and not wanting to be outdone boasted that he could do three. He prepared himself then off he went. He completed the first, then the second, but on the third his right arm weakened and he crumpled into a heap on the grass. Feea burst out into hoots of laughter and started clapping his hands; much to the annoyance of the lad, who was standing, red faced, with a look that was a mixture of embarrassment and anger; a look that said, "How dare anyone laugh at me." The other children were trying not to laugh as he marched over to Feea and stood towering above him; he looked down and spoke with a degree of menace in his voice.

"Who do you think you are laughing at?..What's your name?" he growled.

"Me is Feea," the little lad answered between laughs.

"Well…Feea…did you think that was funny?" the boy said chewing his words.

"Och aye it wis a gid wan awe richt," Feea retorted, trying to control his mirth but failing miserably; the boy was fuming.

"Do you think that you could do any better?" he said through gritted teeth. Feea smiled and answered in his inimitable way.

"Och aye me kin tummel ower ma wulkies awe richt." The boy looked confused.

"You can what?" he asked then without waiting for the answer continued.

"Well if you think that you are so smart let me see you try and do three cartwheels; little did he know that he was in the presence of a champion 'wulkie tumbler'.

Without hesitation, Feea got to his feet, pulling off his jacket and dropping it on the grass. He then, effortlessly performed six perfect cartwheels and as an encore rolled head over heels another six times and landed on his feet. He stood with feet apart, hands on his hips and a broad grin on his face. The three children standing near the wall started cheering and clapping, much to the annoyance of the taller boy, who in a fit of rage and jealousy, kicked Feea's jacket aside and stormed off in a huff. When Feea saw the boy leave, he went back to where he had been sitting and as he bent down to pick up his jacket, he heard the sound of a piper. With his jacket slung over his shoulder and carrying his shoes by the laces, he made his way to the source of the music.

He went round to the back of the house, where most of the guests were; the back green was enormous. There must have been a hundred or more guests mingling around the well kept lawn. There were tables and benches and in the centre was a raised platform with some musicians preparing to play. Feea's eyes lit up when he saw who it was. He couldn't believe it, it was Jamie and the other members of the group along with some others whom he did not recognise; obviously they had been hired to entertain the wedding guests. No sooner had the piper finished when Jamie started singing 'The Piper O' Dundee'; this was more like it. Feea pushed his way through the crowd and stood at the front, waving at Jamie.

The singer saw him but didn't recognise him for a moment, then on realising who it was, smiled. He gestured with his head to the other musicians and on recognising who it was gave a little wave as they continued with the song. Feea noticed the two girls, who he had seen at the wall. They were doing a little dance near the platform; that was Feea's cue. He dropped his jacket and shoes then went over and started to dance with them, but it was his kind of dancing. The girls tried to keep up with him but eventually they moved back and watched in amazement as he pranced and pirouetted round the platform; it was as if his feet were hardly touching the ground. The crowd grew silent as they looked on in awe at this little boy showing such incredible agility. They applauded every amazing leap and spin. The first song was followed by 'Son O' Mars', 'Aitken Drum' and 'Gallawa' Hills'. When they started 'Melville Castle' many of the ladies began to dance. They spun in their flowing dresses and made lines of spinning, vibrant colour that looked like lanes in which Feea danced up and down.

When the dance was finished everyone applauded and cheered Feea; that included the musicians. Feea seamed to be the apple of everyone's eye that day; that is all except one little lad who was still sulking in a corner.

When the festivities were over, William gave Feea a little parcel of tit-bits, as promised and as he said goodbye and reminded him to be at the Cross in three weeks time so that they could go to Craigavon.

Feea kissed his hand and thanked him in his own inimitable way, then the coach that he had arrived in, took him back to the Cross. As Feea walked down the Saltmarket, he drew some strange glances from the passers-bye; they had never seen him in a suit and wearing shoes, that was a sight to behold indeed. Feea found Scruff and they went to his secret place in the stable where he fell asleep listening to the little dog eating his own little banquet.

# CRAIGAVON

It had been three weeks since the wedding and, true to his word; William arrived at the Cross to pick up Feea and Scruff. He looked over and saw them sitting against a wall near the Tollbooth. Feea's clothes looked a bit worse for wear and he was carrying his shoes in his hand. The coach pulled up in front of them and William got out. When Feea saw him he jumped to his feet and ran over to greet him.

"It's a fine day Feea, are you ready for your little adventure," William said with a broad smile on his face.

"Och aye me is ready awe richt, me an' Scruff, he answered excitedly.

"Well climb on board then" William said, pointing to the coach.

Feea didn't need to be told twice, hurriedly he climbed into the coach followed by Scruff and William.

The coachman held the door open for them and when he was satisfied that his passengers were safely on board, secured it and climbed back up into the driver's seat and with a crack of the whip, they were off.

The coach rumbled through the streets and out passed the village of Grahamstown as they headed west into the countryside. They passed the villages of Anderstown and Partick, and then on past farms and woodlands. They forded streams and crossed over creaking bridges on their way to Craigavon Estate; The estate lay between the Campsie Hills and the town of Dumbarton. The old town has a castle perched high up on a rock, looking out over the Clyde estuary; the castle was the former stronghold of the early Britons. The stretch of water beneath the castle was where the inventor Henry Bell conducted trials on his famous ship, 'The Comet', which was to become the World's first ocean going steamship.

Feea had his head stuck out of the window, admiring the scenery for most of the way, while Scruff lay sleeping on the coach floor. They travelled for miles, over hill and dale until they arrived at two huge wrought-iron gates with the name 'Craigavon Castle' written across the top in bold iron letters. The coachman climbed down and pushed them open. He then led the horses inside and closed the gates behind him before climbing back on board and setting off through the estate.

William sat and watched Feea. He smiled at his youthful enthusiasm and the excitement that shone in his eyes. It reminded him of his own youth and the day he got his first pony. He remembered the sheer ecstasy that he felt when he sat in the saddle for the first time and how, with bated breath and pounding heart, he held the reins tightly as his father led the docile animal round the field at the back of the castle. Those were happy days when the sun seemed to shine from dawn to dusk and everyone was smiling and laughing. His smile froze for a second as, in his minds eye, he saw the vision of his mother standing on the veranda waving to him and he, being too scared to let go of the reins, couldn't wave back. She looked so beautiful and elegant that day. The breeze caused her soft flowing dress to hug her tall, sylph like body and sent the gossamer like material billowing out from her shoulders like the wings of an angel. William's mother had been a wonderful woman whose very presence had filled the house with joy. She always seemed to be surrounded by an aura of love that reached out and gave you a feeling of tranquillity as it held you in its gentle embrace. She was always there to help when any of the families who lived on the estate, had a problem. They looked on her as someone that they could trust and rely on.

When she died, it was as if a light had gone out and plunged Craigavon and all who lived there into a dark despair from which his father never recovered. Although he had married late in life to a girl some thirty years his junior, the love and affection that he held for her was the driving force in his life and the terrible pain that he felt in his heart with her departure, was more than his mind could take. The only escape from his un-consolable grief was in the realms of a fantasy that took the shape of an imaginary war. This war was very real to him, it was a battle for his life and the enemy, who was ever trying to encroach on his sanctuary, was reality itself.

To his troubled mind, the world outside Craigavon Castle was a battlefield and the Castle had to be defended at all costs. He believed that his imaginary forces were billeted in the grounds of the estate and their front line was holding the enemy at bay.

William's father, who had been a Colonel in the army, was Laird of Craigavon; a title that had been handed down through generations and one that William, being the eldest son, would inherit in due course. The old Colonel had been retired from the services due to his state of mind. He was a huge, bulk of a man with a perfectly shaped handlebar moustache that curled back towards his ears. Tam, the ghillie on the estate, had been his batman for almost thirty years and had retired about the same time as the Colonel. Old Tam had a great respect for the Colonel and felt a deep sorrow for how life had treated him in his latter years. Tam remembered how proud and elegant the Colonel had been and hated to see him in his present condition; yet, even he, like the rest of the servants and workers on the estate, played along with the Colonel's fantasies and would never let anyone ridicule him.

This tragic and, sometimes comic, state of affairs had prevailed for almost twenty years at Craigavon.


The sun danced through the trees as the coach made its way along the rugged path that would eventually lead to the main house; Craigavon Castle. The castle had been built in the latter part of the seventeenth century and had been modified over the years.

The estate stretched for miles in every direction, taking in farms, woodland, towering crags and a loch that lay to the west of the castle. The River Leven, which contained a fine stock of salmon, made its meandering way through the estate, almost cutting it in half.

Being mid-summer, the estate was in full bloom. The rhododendron bushes were a profusion of colours that ranged from the purest white to the deepest red. The animals that seemed to be everywhere fascinated Feea, there were cows, sheep, deer, pigs, horses and every kind of fowl from chickens to geese. William smiled at the look of amazement on the little boy's face, as he excitedly looked out of one side of the coach then dashed across to look out of the other. He had never seen anything like it. To his eyes, it was a veritable wonderland of animals and birds. This was very different to the squalid surroundings that he was used to.

Eventually the coach pulled up in the covered entrance to the castle, which stood with its twin turrets pointing up towards a cloudless sky. A footman called James opened the coach door and Feea stepped down followed by Scruff and William. William then introduced Feea to James. James eyed the little lad up and down. He was quite shocked at the little boy's dirty face and matted hair; and not, quite knowing what to make of his unusual manner of walking. They made their way through the front door and into a magnificent entrance hall that had an elegant marble stairway with oil paintings on the wall leading up to the first floor.

Feea was fascinated with the suits of armour that were standing by the sides of the doors in the grand hall. They looked like soldiers on guard duty.

Meanwhile, Scruff was sniffing everything that he could see, and, deciding that he had found what he was looking for and started to relieve himself against the leg of one of the suits of armour. Feea ran over and tried to stop him as William burst out laughing.

"That's the funniest thing that I've seen in years," he said, slapping his thigh. "There are far too many of those things in the house, they are everywhere. That's a worthy criticism of the over-elaborate décor."

"I'll see to it sir," the footman said as he dashed into the kitchen to fetch one of the under-house maids. Feea took a piece of twine that he kept in his pocket and put it round Scruff's neck like a collar and led him back out of the door.

"Me be back in a minute," he said as he dragged the little dog out into the grounds. William couldn't stop laughing as he watched them disappear out the front door. The footman returned with a young girl who was carrying a cloth. He showed her where the little dog had done its business. The maid wiped it clean before returning to the kitchen. Feea came back with Scruff on the end of the piece of twine.

"Him no dae it again, he no' know thit it wis yours," he said apologetically.

"Don't concern yourself over it; we have people here to take care of any little mishaps like that. Come and we'll see if we can find something for you to eat, you must be famished." He turned to the footman;

"Go and tell cook to prepare something for my guest and I; we'll be out on the terrace." The footman hurried back to the kitchen as William led Feea down the hall and out onto a terrace that looked over the magnificent grounds at the back of the great house. They sat down at a table. One of the maids came forward and curtsied;

"Would you like something to drink sir?" she asked with a lilt in her voice that was indicative of someone from the Western Isles.

"Yes," William answered, "bring me a brandy and some lemon water for my friend and maybe you could bring some water and a small bowl for his little dog as well." The maid curtsied again and went back inside.

"Well, Feea, what do you think of Craigavon? Isn't it beautiful?" William said, as he proudly, looked out over the grounds.

"Och aye it is that aw richt Mister Sir," Feea answered thinking that with everybody calling his friend sir, that must be his name. William looked puzzled at this unusual form of address but chose to ignore it, thinking that maybe he didn't hear Feea correctly. The maid returned carrying a tray with two glasses, a decanter, two jugs and a bowl for Scruff. After serving them and leaving the containers on the table, she made her exit. Feea tied the end of the twine that served as a leash for Scruff, round the leg of the chair that he was sitting on, and then he took a sip of the lemon water. He screwed up his face for a second then smiled, "This is better than sugar-ally watter," he thought to himself and took a gulp.

"Does that taste nice?" William asked as he watched the little lad gulping it down.

"Och aye it awfae good; an' it clamps yer jaws in tae," Feea added with a wry smile.

"Well help yourself to some more, there's plenty." Feea didn't need a second telling. He reached out and using both hands proceeded to drink straight from the jug. But in his exuberance, he tipped it up too far causing the liquid to go up his nose and spill all over his jacket as he coughed and spluttered while gasping for air. William almost choked on his brandy as he tried to refrain from laughing.

"It's better to use the glass," he quipped with a friendly nod as Feea tried to rub the lemon water off his saturated jacket.

"Me didnae ken thit it wid dae that," Feea said apologetically, once he had composed himself.

"What are we going to do with you?" William jovially exclaimed, then they both burst out laughing.

The maid arrived with a food trolley and after cleaning and setting the table, dished the food out. It consisted of cold meat, potatoes, boiled carrots and peas. She poured some hot gravy over the meat and placed a bowl of fruit in the middle of the table. Before putting some scraps down for Scruff and making her exit. Feea sat, staring with his mouth open, at the banquet in front of him.

"Well, what are you waiting for? Tuck in," William said, picking up his knife and fork. Without hesitation, Feea grabbed at the food with both hands and started to stuff it into his mouth causing his cheeks to bulge. William was taken aback with the young lad's uncouth table manners. He decided to try to teach him a more acceptable way of eating.

"It's better if you use your knife and fork," he said with a knowing smile. Feea looked, blankly, at him.

"Those things there," William said, pointing to the implements at either side of Feea's plate. The little lad looked just as blankly at them; he had never used a knife and fork in his life, so he just sat there, looking down at the strange objects, half expecting them to do something.

"Like this," William said as he demonstrated their use. Feea picked them up and fumbled with them in his food, knocking most of it on to the table. After a few minutes of chasing a pea round his plate and continuing the chase onto the table, William gave up and told him to eat the way that he knew best.

Feea put the knife and fork down and ate the food that he had spilled onto the table with his fingers; including the illusive pea.

When they had finished eating, William suggested that Feea should have a bath before being introduced to the 'Colonel'. He told the boy about the Colonel's idiosyncrasies by saying that the old man liked to play at soldiers.

William called a maid and instructed her to take Feea up to the bathroom and bath him.

When Feea had been washed and suitably attired, William took him upstairs to his father's study. He knocked on the door and entered. The old Colonel was sitting over at the window and when he saw his son standing at the door with Feea, got up and went over to greet them.

"Ah, a new recruit I see, welcome on board," he said holding out his hand in greeting. Feea bent forward and kissed it, not quite the reaction that the old man had expected. He stepped back and with a 'Humph', looked down at Feea.

"Oh, I see, you're a Dandy are you? well we'll soon knock that out of you; you're in the army now, you know, spit and polish and jankers for the lower ranks; what do you say to that, eh?"

Feea nodded and smiled; not understanding a word that the old Colonel had said. The Colonel turned to William.

"Right captain, I think you should get this young recruit billeted and see to it that he reports to me in the morning; you are dismissed." And with that he turned and made his way back over to the window where he picked up a spyglass and looked out over the estate. William left with Feea; making sure that he closed the study door behind him.

Over the next few days Feea and the Colonel grew very fond of each other. They would be seen parading back and forth along the veranda outside the Colonel's study. Feea would be carrying a piece of wood that he held over his shoulder like a rifle, with the Colonel marching at his side with his baton under his arm, giving instructions; they were a comical sight to behold, with the Colonel talking all sorts of military jargon and Feea not understanding a single word of it, but they were both having a great time. Every now and then the Colonel would send Feea on a reconnaissance mission to the edge of the wood where the old officer would watch him through his spyglass. Feea's mission was to report if there was any enemy movement in the area. Of course Feea didn't know what he was looking for and instead would go off, chasing rabbits at the edge of the trees. These playful encounters would take place at the weekend as Feea was given the task of helping Tam the guillie and looking after the stables; a job that he loved because it made him feel at home with the horses. So this was the life that the little lad was settling into; he had never been happier and he even got used to wearing shoes; but his adventure was just beginning.

## INFERNO

Feea had just finished mucking out the stables when Tam appeared carrying a 'gin-trap'.

"They're at it agi'n, damned poachers," he cursed, throwing the object into a corner. "Yae'll hae tae come wae me an' see if we kin find onay mair o' they vile contrapchuns. Ah know thit it's that Ben Cullen, an' wan o' these days am gonnae catch him, an' God help him when ah dae."

"Kin we tak' Scruff wae us?" Feea asked.

"Naw, we had better leave him in his wee pen, jist incase he gets himself caught in wan o' they things," Tam said crossing over to the workbench and picking up a piece of rope. He put it in a sack then turned to Feea. "Run up tae the big hoose an ask Mrs Paton tae fix us a snack tae tak' wae us, fur we'll be awa a' day."

Feea ran up to the house while Tam put some more bits and pieces in the sack. He took out his knife to check that it was sharp before replacing it in the sheath that hung from the side of his belt, then he went outside just as Feea arrived, carrying some food wrapped up in a piece of linen. Tam took it from him and put it in the sack with the rest of the stuff, before they set off towards the woods.

As they crossed the bridge over the waterfall, Feea looked over the side and was fascinated with the scene below him. The spray from the cascading water had caused a mist to rise up with rainbow patterns appearing and disappearing as a breeze caused it to drift over to the far bank where it vanished in the bushes. "Come on, what's keepin' ye!" Feea looked up to see that Tam was shouting at him from the other side of the bridge. He ran across to join him before entering the woods. Tam picked up two pieces of branch, and after pruning the leaves and twigs from them, kept one and handed the other to Feea.

"Use this tae prod the grun' before ye pit your fit doon, jist in case there is wan o' they traps ready to go aff; dae it like this," Tam said, prodding the deep grass in front of them. Feea copied him as they progressed into the undergrowth. The old ghillie appeared to know where he was going as they went deeper into the woods.

The cawing of a crow echoed through the tall pine trees as they approached the centre. High above their heads, the pine branches had become intertwined and formed a canopy that was so thick, the sunlight couldn't penetrate it. The result was, that not only was this part of the wood in semi-darkness, nothing would grow on the ground either. The floor was a carpet of pine twigs and cones that crunched and snapped as Tam and Feea made their prodding way into the heart of the forest. Every now and then, their attention would be drawn to the snapping of a twig and the light padding of hooves, as a young deer would dart through the undergrowth in its haste to escape from the interlopers who had invaded its territory.

There was a loud metallic clank as Tam prodded the twigs in front of him. He lifted the branch that he was using as a prod to reveal the trap that was clamped onto the end of it. The trap was tied to a tree with a piece of twine so that the animal, most probably a deer, couldn't escape. Feea ran over to see what had made the noise.

"Be careful laddie there's boun' tae be mer o' these things aboot." Tam said. He pulled his prod from the jaws of the trap and placed the cruel contraption back in its hiding place, only this time it was harmless. They separated and continued to prod the ground. Feea almost jumped out of his skin when his prod made contact with a trap and as it snapped shut, the force nearly wrenched his pole from his hands. He tried to extract it from the trap but the metal teeth had embedded themselves into the wood. Tam came over when he saw Feea struggling. He forced his prod into the trap and wedged it open, releasing Feea's, which had its end almost bitten off.

"That could 'ave bin yer leg," he said shaking his head and gritting his teeth.

"Me gote a fright when it banged," Feea exclaimed, blowing air between his puckered lips in a silent whistle. They continued their search and found another three traps. It had taken most of the day and it was starting to get dark. They sat down to eat their snacks.

"Now we'll hae tae wait an' see who turns up," Tam said, lying back against a fallen tree trunk.

"Wull the bad mannies come?" Feea asked, looking around.

"Och aye, they'll be back tae check thur traps; bit we'll be ready fur them. So keep yer een open."

The old man dozed while Feea kept watch. Feea sat and listened to the sounds that seemed to be all around him. He could hear the wood pigeons fluttering in the trees above his head and the familiar sound of the fawns padding about among the trees. After a few hours, when it was dark, he heard the hooting of an owl somewhere in the gloom and the cry of a fox that was lurking nearby in the undergrowth. As he looked around a flickering light caught his eye, it seemed to be a long way off and kept appearing and disappearing amongst the trees, as it got closer. He shook old Tam; who was snoring his head off.

"Whit! Whit is it!" He grunted, shaking his head, in an attempt to clear the sleep away.

"Me see sumthin' oot ther'. It's a licht gawn oan an' aff," Feea said excitedly, pointing into the darkness. Tam looked in the direction that Feea was pointing but saw nothing. He was just about to scold the lad for waking him up when he saw it. It was just a flicker some way off but enough to tell him that the poachers were coming back. He told Feea to hide in the undergrowth while he ducked behind a tree and waited. They heard the crunching of twigs as the poachers got closer, then, just as they were level with the tree that Tam was behind, the old ghillie jumped out;

"DINNA MOVE!" he shouted. One of the poachers took off, back the way he had come. The other turned and threw his lantern at Tam before running off in a different direction. The lantern missed Tam and smashed against a tree, causing the burning oil to set light to the piles of tinder dry twigs and branches that were scattered around. They burst into flames that started to spread. Feea came out from his hiding place and ran to Tam's side. The ghillie was trying to stamp out the flames but it was hopeless, the fire had taken hold and was threatening to overwhelm them. Tam grabbed his sack and, pointing to a gap in the trees, told Feea to run towards the river. Feea didn't need a second telling and was off like a shot with Tam hurrying on behind. Feea heard a snap and a scream; he turned to see Tam writhing about on the ground with a huge wall of flame right behind him. He ran back to see what had happened. The old man's foot was caught in one of the traps that they had missed and not only was his ankle broken but the trap was tied to a tree with thick twine.

"The knife!" the old man gasped, "tak' ma knife an' cut the twine...cut the tw...." Then he collapsed. Feea tried to waken him but to no avail. He took the knife from the ghillie's belt as burning embers started to rain down on them. With one stroke, he cut through the thick twine.

By now, the heat was intense and the flames were threatening to engulf them. There wasn't a minute to lose, he took the rope from the sack and tied it round the old man. Then he started to drag him through the undergrowth in an effort to get away from the unbearable heat. The sound of sparking and cracking was deafening as Feea strained on the rope. He pulled and hauled the unconscious man as the fire and smoke started to encircle them and threatened to cut off their only means of escape. He gasped for air as the choking smoke filled his nostrils, causing him to cough and splutter. Feea strained his streaming eyes to see where he was going but all he could see was thick smoke and beyond that, the orange glow of the flames, his situation was hopeless. Burning branches were snapping and falling all around him as the fire leapt from tree to tree.

His head was spinning and he was on the point of collapse, when, out of the smoke came a terrified deer that ran past him in its panic to get away from the inferno. This gave Feea fresh hope and he summoned up the energy for one last effort. He started to drag Tam in the direction the deer had taken; hoping that its instinct was better than his. He could taste the burning timber, as every gasping breath scorched the back of his throat. His smoke- blackened face was streaked with the tears that were streaming from his smarting eyes as he pulled and dragged the unconscious ghillie.

Just he was about to give up, he lost his footing and went tumbling down an embankment, dragging Tam with him. They landed in a heap at the side of the river. Feea scrambled to his feet and as far as he could see, the fire was blazing along the length of the river in both directions with burning branches and trees falling onto the bank. Their only means of escape was to get across to the other side, where there were open fields. This was the narrowest part of the river with rocks and boulders breaking the surface either side of the fast flowing current in the middle. Feea decided to get the trap off Tam's foot, before attempting to get him over to the other side.

He grabbed the tooth-like jaws with both hands and pulled as hard as he could. Slowly they began to open. He tugged and strained at the trap and as soon as it was clear of the old man's foot, he threw it to the side, where it landed with a snap as it sprang shut. Blood started to flow from the wound. Feea dragged the old man out onto the rocks, just in time to get clear of a flaming pine tree that came crashing down onto the bank where they had been. Remembering how Mungo the blacksmith had shown him how to cauterise a wound, Feea took the ghillie's knife and went over to the fallen tree. He put the blade of the knife into the glowing embers and when it was red-hot, went back and held it against the deep gash on the old man's ankle, causing the flow of blood to stop.

Back at the castle, the crackling and crashing that was coming from the forest had awoken the Colonel. He got up and went over to the bedroom window. He pulled back the drapes and gasped at the sight that met his eyes. The panoramic scene was of billowing smoke and flaming trees.

"A second front," he gasped. He grabbed his sword and ran out onto the veranda, fumbling with his sword-belt as he tried to get it round his billowing nightshirt.

"A second front! They're trying to open a second front!" he shouted down to the servants, who were standing, looking at the fire. "Get a message to the third field-battery, tell them to open fire on the enemy's flanks and tell my officers to report to me immediately. They won't catch us napping, not The Fifth, they won't," and with that, he ran inside to consult his maps.

Meanwhile, clouds of choking smoke billowed across the river as the wind changed direction, causing sparks and embers to rain down on the boulders and rocks that were scattered along that side of the riverbank. The river was shimmering in the glow from the fire. Feea looked at the fast flowing water and the rocks that were on the other side, some twenty feet away and realized that there was no time to waste; he had to get help for Tam. He looked at the gap between the rocks and remembered how he could jump across Glassford Street. The surfaces might have been different but the distance was about the same. He took his shoes off and threw them over to the other side, where they landed near a bush. Then he checked that Tam was in a comparatively safe position, before taking a few steps back towards the flaming trees. He felt the heat on his back, as he got ready to make his run. Then he took off, splashing through the pools of warm ash covered water and leapt across the gap but all the effort that he had used dragging Tam through the woods, had drained his energy, causing him to land short of his target and into the midst of the fast flowing current. He splashed about in a wild panic as it carried him downstream towards the waterfall and certain death. The undercurrents tried to drag him down as he gasped for air. Then just as it appeared that all was lost, a huge pine tree came crashing down about fifty yards downstream and almost bridged the river. The water soon extinguished its flaming branches as Feea went crashing into it. He grabbed hold of a charred branch and held on as the torrent swept over him. He could feel the tree starting to move towards the waterfall. The end of it was only about five feet away from the far bank but as the tree moved, it was turning downstream and the gap was getting wider. Feea scrambled to the end and with all the effort he could muster, he pushed away from the tree and tried to swim towards the bank. Just as he was about to be swept back into the current, his foot touched a rock and without hesitation he used it to propel himself towards the rocks at the side. His fingers managed to grip one and using all his strength, managed to drag himself out of the water and on to the bank where he lay panting for breath.

When he had recovered, he climbed up the embankment and ran towards the farmhouse that was nearby. As he approached, he saw the farm workers standing at the gate watching the fire; he ran up to them.

"Ghillie man, him hurt, ye'll need a rope tae get him!" he shouted. One of the men ran over to a cart and came back with a long piece of rope.

"Where is he?" he asked.

"Me show ye, come oan, hurry," Feea said and started to run back the way he had come. The others followed on behind.

When they arrived at the place where Feea had tried to jump across, the heat was oppressive. There were fallen trees all along the far bank and they were well ablaze.

"Look, he is ther'," Feea said, pointing to the unconscious ghillie lying on the rocks at the other side of the river.

"But we cannae get tae him the river's too wide an that current wid drag ye doon," one of the men said, the others agreed. Then Feea piped up;

"Me kin dae it, me kin loup the watter an' yae kin throw the rope ower tae me." The man carrying the rope turned to Feea.

"Dinna be daft, laddie, nae body kin jump that fawr, an onyhow wae aw that heat an' smoke ower ther', the auld man is likely tae be deed b' noo."

"Naw he no', me wull get him," and with that Feea climbed down the embankment.

"Come back!" the men cried. Feea ignored them. He pushed his back hard against a boulder then lunged forward, picking up speed as he jumped from rock to rock then let fly in a mighty leap across the flowing water; There could be no mistake this time. He landed with a 'plunge,' just short but managed to grab a rock and pull himself up onto the other bank. The men looked on in amazement as he got to his feet. One of the men threw the rope over. Feea took the end and started to tie it onto the shorter one that he had put round Tam when there was the sound of a loud crack right behind him.

"Look out!" the men shouted as a huge pine started to topple forward. It stopped, balancing precariously against another, right above Feea and the ghillie. Sparks and flaming twigs rained down as the lad worked furiously to secure the rope.

"Get oot a ther'!" the men screamed as the flaming tree started to slip

"It ready!" Feea shouted as he pulled Tam to the water's edge.

The men took up the strain on the rope and pulled the ghillie into the water with Feea hanging on to the old man's belt. The current pulled them down stream as the men, hastily moved away just in time as the falling tree came crashing down. The old man started to recover when he hit the water and began to splash about in panic, almost causing Feea to loose his grip. Feea held on as the men pulled them onto the bank. They lifted old Tam and carried him to the farmhouse with Feea trailing along behind.

When they got the old man inside, they laid him down and taking some pieces of wood, made a splint to support his ankle. Then one of the men ran to the Big House to let them know what had happened.

As the man ran towards the house, there was a loud clap of thunder, followed by a downpour of torrential rain, as a thunderstorm erupted. The fork lightening zigzagged across the sky as the relentless downpour extinguished the fire, causing clouds of steam to rise up into the night sky with a prolonged 'hiss' that could be heard throughout the valley.

As he approached the house, he looked up to see the Colonel standing on the veranda outside his bedroom and all he had on was his nightshirt. He stood posing in the torrential rain with his sword held high above his head shouting; "THAT'S IT LADS, GIVE THEM HELL!"

The farm worker could only look up and smile at this incredulous sight. He ran inside and told the butler what had happened to Tam. Then both of them made their way back to the farmhouse with the butler carrying his emergency box of bandages and medicines.

# SCAPEGOAT

Feea held a lantern over old Tam as one of the men put a flask to the ghillie's
lips.

"Tak a sip o' this, it'll wa'rm ye up," the man said as he supported Tam's head
with his free hand.

Just then, the butler arrived and got to work on Tam's, badly swollen ankle.

Tam let out a howl as the butler poured some raw alcohol onto the gash in his
foot.

"Ca' Cannae wae that stuff," he exclaimed then took another gulp from the
flask.

After binding the wound, the small group of men helped the old ghillie back to
his home where his wife waited, anxiously, for his arrival: having been told of
his injury by one of the grounds men,

The old woman got herself into a state of panic and ran over to her husband's
side.

"Are ye a' richt, Tam?" she asked, almost screaming into the old man's ear.

"A'm fine wummin, a'm fine. Dinnae get yersel' intae sich a state." Tam
answered, taking a strong grip of her hand, in order to reassure her.

"Bit the fire, hoo did yea get oot o' that, the hale sky wis lit up wae it?"

"Och it wis wee Feea thit saved me, if it hidna been fur him a'd a been toastit fur
sure," the old man said casting an admiring glance in Feea's direction. "That
wee laddie's a hero. He saved ma life without thinkin' o' his ain."

The old woman went over and gave Feea a hug.

"A cannae thank yae enough laddie; he micht be an owl scunner bit he a' ave
gote," she exclaimed, almost crushing Feea to death.

Feea was a local hero for weeks and was treated with kindness by the estate
workers.

Everything was going well until a nephew of Williams arrived; this was Ewan Caldwell, the twelve-year-old son of William's younger brother James. The young boy was completely spoilt and had to be the centre of attention. This was the boy that Feea had met at the wedding reception and at which meeting Ewan had taken a particular dislike to Feea due to the fact that Feea seemed to be so popular with the guests and had shown him up in front of the children at the wedding. Ewan's jealousy had not abated from that day and when he found out that Feea was on the estate, started to make plans that would turn the family against him; after all, he wasn't even family, so why should this outsider from the lower classes be so popular.

Soon after William had left to do some business in Europe, he set his mischievous plans in motion.

As the weeks passed, things began to go missing, like a pie would mysteriously disappear from the kitchen, or a silver candlestick from the dining room. All manner of things were going missing; admittedly they were small things but it was happening so often that rumours were going around that there was a thief on the estate; and Ewan was not slow in pointing the finger in the direction of Feea. Every time it was mentioned in his company, he would hint that it must be a servant or worker on the estate; obviously someone from the lower classes; someone like Feea for instance. In so doing, he planted the seed of doubt in the minds of, not only the family, but the estate workers as well; they began to look at Feea and wonder. They didn't want to believe it but he was the likeliest candidate; and so the scene was set for the 'coup de grace'; the final nail in Feea's coffin; which was, (the way things turned out), true, in more ways than one. But Feea was totally oblivious to what was going on. He kept himself busy each day by mucking out the stables or walking the horses, then he and Scruff would go and play in the fields. Every Monday morning he would take a basket and go to the henhouse where he would collect the eggs. He'd then take them up to the castle and put them in a bowl on the kitchen table.

For this little task he usually got a piece of shortbread from Tam's wife who would be busy preparing breakfast for the household.

It had been about two months since Feea arrived on the estate and he really loved being there and William had told him on many occasions that he could stay as long as he wanted. He had a bed in a little hut at the back of the stables where he and Scruff slept; this was like Paradise compared to the conditions that he had been living under back in Glasgow. But he did miss the music and the songs that came from the taverns. Some nights he would wander down to where the Gaelic estate workers stayed and as they sang in their huts he would dance alone in the moonlight to songs like 'Chi mi'n Geamhradh' or 'Tog Orm mo Piob'; although he did not know it, these songs were from the part of Scotland where was born; namely The Western Highlands. He liked to keep to himself yet in so doing, led a lonely, but happy life on the estate.

But with the help of Ewan Caldwell, everything was about to change. Ewan kept stealing things and hiding them in his secret hiding place which was under an old tree stump in a part of the woods that had been untouched by the fire. There was a room in the castle that no one but the Colonel was allowed to enter; it was his wife's morning room and in there he kept all her jewellery and other possessions. Everything was just as it was the day she died; it was as if she had never left, except for the dust that had gathered over the years. The old Colonel used to visit this room every morning after breakfast. He would just stand, look around and sigh as the memory of happier times would come flooding back. This was his real sanctuary and every one, including his sons, respected it. Although the door was never locked no one but the Colonel ever entered; that was until that tragic Monday morning.

Ewan knew about the room and how important it was to the Colonel. To him the Colonel was just a silly old man who he had no respect for and ridiculed him at every turn; much to the despair of his father and Uncle William. Unknown to anyone, he had secretly entered the room and knew where everything was.

On that fateful morning he got up and dressed before anyone was awake and silently crept along the corridor. When he got to the room he turned the doorknob and quietly entered. The first rays of dawn were streaming through a chink in the curtain as he crossed to the dressing table. In the gloom he bumped into a chair and stumbled into the dressing table causing some of the items to fall over. He bit his lip and listened to see if anyone had heard but all was quiet. Quickly he grabbed a silver framed miniature portrait of the Colonel's wife and a locket that had been lying in front of it; he put the items in his pocket and silently left the room. He quietly made his way down stairs and out into the grounds. He ran to the woods and put the items with the others that he had collected, then, unobserved he made his way back to the castle and on entering his room and fully clothed, climbed back into bed where he lay listening for the chimes of the grandfather clock down in the entrance hall; when it struck six he knew that Feea and Scruff would be away to collect the eggs from the henhouse. He got up and stealthily crept back to the woods and his hiding place. He collected the items in a cloth and hid in the thicket near the path that led up to the castle. He watched in the direction of the henhouse. The sun was breaking through the morning mist as Feea came into sight. He was carrying the egg basket in one hand and holding a piece of twine that served as a leash for Scruff in the other. As they passed, Ewan ducked down but Scruff was aware that there was someone in the bushes and started to yelp while trying to get to them. "No yelp ur yel wakey every buddy up," Feea said in a hushed voice, while at the same time giving the twine a tug and half dragging the little dog along with him. When they were out of sight, Ewan ran over to Feea's hut and went inside. He looked around for a place to hide the booty. He saw a pile of sacks over by the bed and hurriedly hid the items underneath them. Then he left and got back into the house and up to his room without being seen. He undressed and climbed back into bed where he soon fell asleep.

It was just after breakfast when the Colonel entered the dusty room, when he saw the dressing table and the empty place where his beloved wife's portrait had been, he gasped in horror and hurried over. In a panic he searched the floor and round behind the furniture. On realising that it was gone, he ran towards the door shouting, "Help! Robbers!" In his panic he didn't see the chair that had been moved when Ewan had knocked into it and went tumbling over it, banging his head against the door frame; he collapsed with a heavy thud onto the floor and lay there motionless as James and the servants came hurrying to see what all the commotion was about. When James turned his father onto his back he could see that he was dead.

"Oh no," he sobbed as he cradled the old man in his arms.

The servants helped him to carry the Colonel into his bedroom where they laid him on the bed. Ewan stood at his room door in disbelief at what had happened, a cold shiver ran down his spine when he realised that he alone was responsible for this tragedy; he had to act quickly in order to put the blame on the person that he hated most. Later that day, James and the butler entered the room where the Colonel had died. They looked around but at first didn't see anything out of place, except for the chair that was lying on its side near the door. The butler crossed over to the dressing table and after looking at the surface, called James over.

"Look at this," he said pointing to the marks on the dust covered surface; it was obvious that something had been removed. Then he pointed to a perfect palm print.

"And what do you make of this," he said looking closely at it.

As James looked down at it an angry look came over his face.

"It's a child's, it's a child's hand print," and with that, he turned and quickly left the room. He marched into Ewan's room and confronted him. Ewan looked startled when he saw the look on his father's face.

"Have you been in that room along there, and don't lie to me? There's a child's hand print on the dressing table and you are the only child in this house, he said pointing his finger. Ewan panicked.

"No dad it wasn't me, I would never go in there it was forbidden; you told me so. Honest I've never been in there," he protested.

James went over to the window and looked up at the sky.

"Well if it wasn't you then who was it? You are the only child in this house," he said with a hint of frustration in his voice.

"There's that boy Feea, he was here this morning. I saw him running from the house and I think he had something under his jacket," Ewan said with an innocent look on his face. Slowly his father turned from the window. He stood, quietly looking down at the floor and rubbing his chin. Then he made his way towards the door. Before he left the room, he turned to Ewan.

"You stay here till I get back." He went down the hall and entered the room again where he spoke to the butler.

"Come with me I think we may have an answer to this mystery,"

The butler followed James as he made his way to Feea's hut. The two men entered, Feea stood with a quizzical look on his face as James immediately, started to search. He looked under the bed and on shelves then his eyes settled on the pile of sacks. He threw them to the side exposing the items that Ewan had placed there. As he looked through them, he saw the portrait of his mother. That brought his temper to boiling point.

"You filthy little thief," he growled, grabbing Feea by the throat.

"Me no dae nuthin', me no dae nuthin'," Feea pleaded, totally shocked by the venom in his assailant's voice. Scruff, who had been sleeping on the bed, jumped down and started yelping and biting at James's ankles. The butler threw a sack over the little dog and held him while James dragged Feea outside. When the butler left the hut, he threw Scruff back inside and slammed the door shut. The little dog could be heard yelping and scratching at the door as Feea was dragged by the scruff of the neck towards the stables. When they got there Tam was sweeping the yard. He stopped and went over to see what was going on. The butler told him what they had found in Feea's hut and what had happened to the Colonel. The old man's mouth dropped open in disbelief. The other men bundled Feea into the stable and tied him up in an empty stall. As Feea lay with his hands and feet bound and a gag over his mouth, James spoke to him.

"I'm sending for a constable who will take you and lock you up in Dumbarton Jail and that's where you will stay till you rot."

James and the butler left, telling Tam to watch over their prisoner till the constable arrived. Tam, who was still in shock at the news of his friend's death; slowly wandered into the stable, he pulled a crate over and sat looking down at Feea. The little lad was a pitiful sight lying all trusted up in the corner. Tam reached down and untied the gag.

"Whit hiv yae done laddie," he asked, shaking his head.

"Me didnae dae nuthin', Feea answered. "Nuthin'at a'." Tam looked him straight in the eye.

"Bit whit aboot the stuff that's in yer hut, it didnae get ther' awe bae it'sell', noo did it?"

"It no' mine, me didnae see it ther'." Feea said, shaking his head and looking totally dejected. "Me is no a feef," he added.

"A don't know whit's gawn oan here bit wan thin's certain, A've loast wan gid freen' the day an' am damn sure A'm no gonnae loose twa. Unless A'm a bad judge, A dinna think it's in yae tae tak somthin' that didnae belang tae yae." He started to untie the cord round Feea's wrists and ankles. When he was free Feea threw his arms round Tam's neck and hugged him; the old man patted him on the back.

"Ther' noo you gang awa an' tak' wee Scruff wae ye. Go doon The Leven an' turn left at the Clyde then keep gawn tae yae get tae Glesca; will yae remember that noo."

"Aye me wull dae it," Feea answered and kissed the old man's hand. There was a tear in old Tam's eye as he gave Feea a hug.

"God go wae ye laddie," he whispered, and with that Feea left the stable.

# ESCAPE

Feea took Scruff and made his escape through the fields. He headed for the
river Leven, remembering what Tam had told him about it running into the
Clyde near Dumbarton Castle. He knew that if he followed the Clyde upriver, it
would take him back to Glasgow where he and Scruff would be safe.
Having arrived at the Leven, they made their way downstream towards the
Clyde. It was dark by the time they reached the village of Dumbarton and Feea
was getting hungry. They left the riverside and made their way into the town to
search for something to eat. There was singing and laughter coming from the
Inn as they entered the village. Feea, knowing that there were scraps of food to
be found at the back of the Inns in Glasgow, made his way round to the alley at
the rear of the building. He found a pile of rubbish and started to sift through it
while Scruff sniffed about in the dark recesses. All of a sudden, the back door
of the inn burst open, bathing the area in light, and there, standing in the
doorway was the fat, red faced, Innkeeper. His huge belly was straining to burst
through his apron as he stood with his hands on his hips. He saw Feea and with
a loud bellowing voice, started to shout at him.
"Whit's awe this! Get awa fae ther', we dinna wa'nt beggars roon here; noo get
awa wae ye."
Feea looked up to see the monstrous silhouette standing in the doorway; he
didn't need a second telling and made off along the alley with Scruff, who had a
ham bone in his mouth, hard on his heels. He turned into the Main Street and
sat down at the water trough outside the blacksmiths yard. Scruff sat beside
him, gnawing on the bone while Feea sat there, listening to his stomach
rumbling and looking, longingly at the ham bone that Scruff had trapped
between his paws as he crunched away at it. He reached down and tried to take
it from him but Scruff held it tight between his teeth as he growled. Feea lifted
the bone up with both hands, the little dog was holding on with his teeth as he

was lifted clear of the ground. Feea tried shaking him off but it was no use, the little dog wouldn't let go. He gave up and lowered Scruff back down to the ground with his bone.

"You is too greedy," he said as the dog continued to chew on the bone while keeping an eye on Feea, just in case he should try again.

Just then, a peddler came along the street pushing his barrow. Feea got up, and having taken off his shoes, ran over to him carrying them in his hand,

"Hi mister, dae ye wa'nt tae buy ma shoes?" He said, holding them up to the man. The peddler, who was a shifty looking character, looked at Feea and stopped pushing the barrow.

"Let me hae a luk at thum," he said taking the shoes from Feea. "Thur awfae dirty, a'll gie ye three-happ'ny fur thum," he said with a sneer.

"Me tak' it," Feea said, nodding his head in agreement. The man threw the shoes on the barrow and handed Feea the three coins. He then went on his way giggling to himself. Feea went over to the Inn and went in the front door. He walked up to where the fat innkeeper was serving and put the three coins on the bar.

"Kin me get somthin' tae eat fur that", he said, with a look of expectation in his eyes. The fat man glowered down at him.

"Three happnies, whit dae ye expect tae get fur that?"

"Me is awfae hungry fur sumthin tae eat," Feea said, rubbing his tummy. The man took the coins and went through to a room at the back of the Inn. When he came back he was holding three badly bruised apples, he handed them to Feea, who took his hand and tried to kiss it in gratification. The innkeeper drew it back quickly, thinking that the boy might be hungry enough to take a take a bite out of him. Feea slipped the apples into his shirt and ran out into the street. He started to eat them as he made his way back to the river with Scruff trailing on behind with his bone. They entered a grove and Feea sat down under a tree to eat his apples while Scruff sat on the grass chewing away at his bone. When he was finished eating, Feea lay back and fell asleep.

The morning chorus was in full voice with the crows taking a leading part as Feea rubbed his eyes before looking at the sunrise through the trees. He noticed the red objects hanging from the trees, and, on closer inspection, saw that they were apples. He had fallen asleep in an orchard and was surrounded by thousands of them, they were scattered everywhere on the ground. The irony was that he had sold his shoes for three rotten apples only to wake up to more than he could possibly eat in a lifetime and they were all there for the taking. He picked up as many as he could carry, stuffing them into his shirt and pockets. Then he and Scruff made their way back to the river and continued their journey to the Clyde where they turned left and made their way towards Glasgow.

## THE COMET

The sun was beating down as Feea walked along the river bank. He sat down on a rock and looked across the river towards the hills that rose up from the village of Port Glasgow; which was a landing stage for the great sailing ships that came from all corners of the globe. He watched as a tall ship made its way into the port and wondered about what exotic cargo it might be bringing to Scotland. Mostly, it would have been nothing more exotic than tobacco or cotton from the Americas or tea from the Far East. As he watched, another ship was leaving and sailed, majestically, passed the first one as it manoeuvred into position. While he was watching the ships, his attention was drawn to a noise that seemed to be coming from the far side of Dumbarton Rock. As he watched a strange vessel appeared from behind the old fortress. Feea stared at the weird craft as it made its, slow, 'chugging' way up river. It had a tall, metal chimney with thick black smoke pouring out of it. Feea was totally fascinated by this weird looking boat and the strange noises that were coming from it. Scruff started to yelp and run back and forth at the waters edge.

As the vessel got closer, the chugging got erratic and then stopped, with a cloud of black smoke descending down over the deck. As it started to drift, a man's voice shouted to Feea.

"Sonny! Can you catch this rope and secure it to a rock."

Feea looked towards the craft and saw that there were two men onboard. One of the men threw a rope that landed at his feet. He picked up the end and ran over to a large rock, where he secured it. The rope soon became taught as the boat drifted downstream, before stopping and lodging itself sideways on a sandbank, some forty yards out. As the water was very shallow at this side of the sandbank, Feea decided to wade out and look at the strange craft.

He called over to the men as he got near.

"Kin me see yer boat mister?"

"Climb on board," one of the men said, without looking up from what he and the other man were working at.

Feea climbed up the rope and onto one of the paddle-boxes before stepping onto the deck. Both of the men were working away at a contraption near the centre of the boat. Feea went over to see what they were doing.

One of the men had an iron bar and was trying to wedge it between the bulkhead and a conglomerate of iron rods and cog-wheels. The other was trying to get a tool down into the same gap in an attempt to make an adjustment as the boat began to list in the ebbing tide. Meanwhile Scruff had settled down on the riverbank and was dozing in the sun. Feea sat, cross-legged on the deck and watched the men as they worked away. There was a grinding noise as the vessel settled on the sandbank. It tilted at a slight angle as it rested on one of its paddle wheels. Feea looked over the side and watched a school of little fish darting about in the murky water. He reached down and tried to catch one, but as soon as his hand touched the water, they disappeared. He heard a 'clunk' as the men managed to get the part that they were working on, back into place.

"We'll have to wait for the tide to turn before we can try it out," one of the men exclaimed. Feea looked over to see the taller of the two wiping his oily hands on a piece of cloth. The man called over to him.

"Would you like some tea, laddie?" Feea nodded his head and smiled. He had never tasted tea but he wasn't one to refuse an offer, no matter what it was. The other man came over and sat down.

"What's your name lad?" he asked, rubbing his hands on a cloth.

"Me is Feea, an' him ower ther' is Scruff," Feea said, pointing over to the little dog sleeping on the riverbank.

"I'm pleased to meet you Feea, my name is Henry," the man said, shaking the boy's hand.

"It's a braw boat you've gote, bit it mak's some funny noeyses," Feea said with a quizzical look on his face.

"Ah, that's because it's driven by steam," Henry said pointing to the engine.

"Come and I'll show you how it works," he said, getting up and crossing to the contraption at the centre of the deck.

Feea followed him and stood at his side while the inventor explained the mechanism. Feea stood open-mouthed as the man went on about pressure valves, release valves, drive shafts and cogs of every size: not to mention pressure gauges, paddles and the conversion of water into energy through steam. This was all miles above the little lad's head.

"Dis that mak' it go 'puff-puff' then?" Feea asked in all innocence.

"Puff- puff?" the inventor mimicked with a blank expression on his face. "It does a lot more than 'puff-puff,' he said with a smile and a shake of his head. Yet, with all the hard work and ingenuity that went into the inventing and building of the engine, at the end of the day, Feea's simple logic was right; it did make it go 'puff-puff'.

The other man came over carrying three tin mugs, he handed one to Henry and put one down beside Feea.

"Now, be careful, it's hot", he said as he sat down on the deck with his back against the rail that ran round the small ship.

"This is Feea," Henry said, gesturing towards the young boy.

"How do you do Feea?" the man said without giving his own name.

"Me is fine," Feea answered with a smile and cautiously took a sip of his tea. He didn't like it much, so he put it back down on the deck and looked over the side to see if the little fish had come back, but alas, all he could see was the seaweed, swaying to and fro in the silent depths. They sat and talked about the ship and how it was named after a heavenly body called a comet that happened to be in the sky when they were building it. Feea was fascinated with the idea that a star could move across the sky. He told them about his life in Glasgow and his adventures at Craigavon and why he had to leave. The men sympathised with his plight and offered him and Scruff a trip up the river to Glasgow as they were going there to prepare The Comet for her maiden voyage, but first they would have to wait for the tide to turn. They spent the time cleaning and polishing the craft. Feea had the job of cleaning the brass handles, which he did with a touch of exuberance that made them shine like gold. Later in the afternoon, Feea went ashore and untied the rope before collecting Scruff from the riverbank and lifting him on board. The little dog ran about the deck sniffing every part of the ship before settling down near the stern where Henry had put some scraps of food down for him.

Just before twilight, Feea stood between the two men, as all three of them looked downstream towards the town of Greenock. They stood in awe at the sight before them. The Clyde looked like a river of gold as the sun sank into its fiery cauldron.

The stillness of the moment was interrupted by the sound of creaks and groans, as, slowly and unabated; the tide came in and began to lift the small ship off the sandbank. The men stoked the fire in the engine then they grabbed long poles and wedging them between the hull and the sandbank, started to push the ship away from the sloping sand. It was hard work but it soon paid off with the ship drifting away into deeper water. Henry worked at the engine and before long it was hissing and puffing, much to the annoyance of Scruff who started yelping and running back and forth, as if to challenge the metal monster to a fight. Feea and the men laughed at the antics of the little dog. Henry moved a lever and the paddles started to turn, causing the ship to move forward. Feea looked over the side and was fascinated by the way the paddles churned the water into foam that streaked out behind the small ship as it made its way up the river.

Feea did a little dance and mimicked the puffing and hissing sounds as the craft ploughed its way through the water. The men turned and smiled at the scene of the little boy dancing round the deck while his dog was yelping its head off as it challenged the engine.

Slowly the Comet made its way up the Clyde passed the village of Bowling and on towards the village of Clydebank, on it's way to Glasgow. Henry decided that, as it was getting quite dark, they should pull in at Clydebank rather than take the risk of getting stuck on another sandbank further up the river. They pulled in at a jetty and tied up for the night.

The clouds in the evening sky gave way to a clear, starry night. The men went on shore to visit one of Henry's friends, leaving Feea and Scruff to keep an eye on the Comet.

Feea sat back on the deck and looked up at the heavens in the hope of seeing one of the moving stars that Henry had named the strange boat after. He looked up passed the tall funnel and gazed at the myriad of stars that filled the night sky and wondered where they all came from and just what they were. He imagined that maybe the night sky was a giant canopy with lots of little holes in it and that the sun was still shining on the other side. Or maybe it was sparks from a big fire and they had got stuck on the roof of the night sky.

As fanciful as his thoughts may have been, they were no more ridiculous than the fanciful ideas of the great men of the past who looked up into the heavens and saw a bear, a lion, a ram, a bull and a dog; along with some other weird and wonderful creatures. To them, the night sky was some kind of celestial zoo and the whole thing was going round the sun on a gigantic solar merry-go-round. When you think about it in these more enlightened times; Feea's, all too simple idea, of the universe being created with sparks from a great fire, wasn't far from the truth.

As he gazed up into the heavens, something caught his eye. It was only a fleeting glimpse and looked like a streak of light hurtling to earth. He got very excited and jumping to his feet, scoured the sky in the hope of seeing it again.

But everything was still, except for the twinkling of the stars that were nearest the horizon. He was convinced that he had seen a comet and couldn't wait to tell Henry. He spent the next two hours peering up into the night-sky in the hunt for more of the mysterious objects, but all he got for his diligent search was a stiff neck.

When Henry came back he was carrying some food; Feea ran to meet him; "Ah see'd wan o' they things in the sky, same as the wan thit you saw an' caw'd the boat efter, it wis up ther." He said pointing up into the night sky and, excitedly, tugging at Henry's sleeve.

"Where, exactly, did you see it?" Henry said looking up.

"It wis ower ther," Feea said, pointing west. "It wis ther then it wisnae; it wis awfae fast an' ah only saw it fur a wee bit."

Henry looked up for a moment then turned to Feea.

"What you saw was a meteorite or what is sometimes called a 'Shooting Star'. It is a small piece of material, probably no bigger than a grain of sand. It burns when it enters our atmosphere and appears as a streak of light. A comet on the other hand is gigantic and passes the Earth at a distance of many millions of miles. It is easily identified by its long tail and hangs in the sky for days before disappearing".

"Oh", Feea exclaimed with a blank look on his face, not understanding a word that the inventor had said. He felt as though he had been scolded. "Me jist thoat thit it wis wan", he added with a hint of disappointment in his voice. Henry looked at him and smiled.

"I'm sure you'll see one some day, but for now, I've brought some food and later we'll look for more meteorites; what do you say?" Feea's eyes lit up at the prospect of seeing more of the objects.

"Och aye me an' Scruff wull look fur them wae ye," he said with renewed enthusiasm. Just then the other man returned carrying a small cask of ale that he had bought from the tavern in the village. He put it down on the deck and joined the others. They sat and ate their food. Feea wolfed his down as usual and Scruff finished off the scraps. The men checked that the boat was secure before settling down to finish off the ale. When he was finished, Henry went over to where Feea was sitting looking up into the heavens. He sat down beside him and gazed skyward.

The moon shone like a beacon in the cloudless sky as Henry and Feea searched for shooting stars. All was silent except for the occasional creak from the vessel as it rocked ever so gently, or the 'plop' as a rat entered the water beneath the old jetty.

"THER'!" Feea shouted. Henry swung round just in time to grab the little boy's arm and stop him stepping backwards over the side of the boat.

"Careful, lad, or you'll be in the water." Feea was too intent on staring at the sky, to take much heed of Henry's good advice.

"Och, it's awa agi'n," he muttered.

"Did you make a wish?" Henry asked. Feea looked mystified.

"Me no' ken hoo tae mak' wan o' them," he answered, pursing his lips and shaking his head.

"Well," Henry said, "when you see a shooting star; that's another name for a meteorite, you're supposed to make a wish, it's like a hope, you know, something that you would like to have, or something that you like to happen." Feea thought for a moment.

"Och aye, ye mean like sugar-ally, ur somt'n like that." Henry scratched his head.

"Well…I suppose… yes, something like that, but you should make it something that you really want more than anything, like, something that would make you happy, and hope that it comes true." Feea sat down, deep in thought. Then he sprang to his feet.

"Me know, me know", he said excitedly, "me wa'nts sugar-ally an' candy balls an' lotes mer sweeties an' thit yer boat wull go aw right fur ye, an' thit a kin see ma maw an' da, an'…" Henry cut him off, mid-sentence.

"Hold on laddie, not so fast. You're only supposed to make one wish and anyway, you're not supposed to tell anyone or it won't come true." Feea shrugged his shoulders and sighed.

"Och, next time me is gonnae wish fur lotes a' wishes fur the two o' us," and with that he continued to scour the sky. Henry shook his head and smiled at the little boy's unselfish innocence. After a while Henry went and got some blankets, they wrapped themselves up and soon fell asleep under the star studded canopy of the night sky.

Next day they continued their journey up-river and berthed at the Broomilaw in Glasgow. Feea and Scruff disembarked at the quay and after promising to come and see the inventor again, made their way towards the town centre.

## THE MONUMENT

There was a slight breeze blowing as Feea half-walked and half-skipped, along the Gallowgate; it felt so good to be back to his old haunts. He turned into Charlotte Street; one of the better class streets in the city. He started to do a little dance as he made his way down the street. The Reverend Lockart was making his slow, ponderous way up the street, stopping every now and then to catch his breath. He was a kindly old gentleman who lectured in religion at the Glasgow College. Without looking where he was going, Feea went into a spin and crashed right into the old man, almost knocking him off his feet.

"Hold on young Feea," the old man said, holding the young boy by the shoulders as he regained his balance.

"Feea sorry, me wis dancin', me no see ye," the little boy said apologetically. The old man sat down on a box that had been placed beside a garden wall. Ater he got his breath back he smiled and spoke to Feea.

"And how are you today?" he asked as the little boy did a twirl.

"Feea is fine," the little lad answered, "an' dandy tae," he added with a nod and a smile. The old minister looked puzzled at the boy's antics;

"What, are, you doing?" He asked as the little lad continued his dance.

"Feea is dancin" he did another twirl. "See."

Old Lochart looked even more puzzled.

"But there is no music to dance to?"

Feea answered incredulously; "Feea dances tae the wind. Kin ye no' hear it?"

The old man looked thoughtful as he answered;

"Yes, but I've never thought of the wind as music."

Feea answered with a touch of exasperation in his voice;

"Moosic is IN the wind; Listen." Feea was moving his head from side to side, as he listened to music that only he could hear. "Dae ye hear it? Feea kin hear it an' so kin the flewrs an' the trees." He pointed over to a garden where the flowers and grass were swaying in the breeze. "Look! They dance tae it as weel."

The old man decided to humour Feea. "Oh yes, I see, so they are dancing to the music in the wind. But where does it come from?"

The little boy stood with his hands on his hips, as if he was about to pass on an important piece of information;

" Jamie says it's the moosic o' the mountains an' the wind blaws it through the glens an' a' the wei doon tae Glesca'." The old minister half smiled; "Oh, I see, and Jamie can hear it to?"

Feea nodded excitedly; "Aye, an' so kin Blin' Alick, he kin play it oan his fiddle," he nodded knowingly.

Old Lochart looked puzzled and a little bewildered, he spoke to himself as if in a trance; "He can play it on his fiddle, ah well," he sighed and decided to change the subject. "Tell me, where are you sleeping these days?"

Feea looked from side to side, making sure that he wasn't overheard, he put a finger to his lips and wispered " Shoosh!!! In Mc Gurk's stable." He looked around to make sure that no one had heard his secret. The Reverend Lockart nodded in secret understanding; "Oh, I see. Did you know that the baby Jesus was born in a stable?" Feea looked up in amazement;

" No' McGurk's…me no see a bairn in ther'. A only see the big hoarses, an'
some wee rats tae. Scruff, he no like them at a', he chases thum awa."

"Scruff? Is he one of your street friends?" The old man inquired. Feea answered
as if to scold the old man's ignorance;

"Naw, Scruff is the wee dug thit sties wae me in the stable. He keeps me wa'rm
at nicht."

The old minister continued.

"I see, but I didn't mean McGurk's stable. Jesus was born in a stable a long way
from here. It was in a town called Bethlehem and it was a cold night. I expect
you've had your share of those?" Feea sat down on the ground in front of the
minister. He looked up and smiled;

"Och aye, bit Scruff, him keep me wa'rm noo. That Jesus, did he hae a dug
tae?" The old man smiled at the little boy's innocent ignorance;

"No he didn't have a dog Feea. He slept in a manger and Mary and Joseph
looked after him so that he wouldn't get cold."

"Dugs keep ye wa'rm a' richt, you tell them," Feea interrupted.

The old man was becoming a little irritated as he answered the boy;

"No, Feea, you don't understand. You see, Jesus was born a long time ago, long
before you and I were born…Have you never heard of Jesus Christ?" Feea
thought for a moment, then a look of recognition came over his face;

"Him works doon at the wharf." The old minister looked startled at this amazing
revelation; he raised his voice a little, as he looked directly at Feea;

"Our Lord….Working at the wharf??? What do you mean Feea? That's not
possible. Feea answered in a, matter of fact, way.

" Och aye, he's there a' richt, bit a' dinna ken fur hoo lang. Ye see he's aye
dae'n daft things an' he's never oan time fur his work." The old minister, who
was, now lost in the conversation, rushed to the Lord's defence, he was almost
choking as he spoke;

"Dae'n daft things! Never oan time! Wha…" Feea interrupted him; "Aye, an'
he mak's an awfy mess as weil."

Old Lockart could contain himself no longer. He rose to his feet, and, adopting the posture of a barrister defending his client in court, spoke with a loud, clear voice;

"Slander!...Lies... Who would dare to say such things! I put it to you that the Lord was standing at those gates long before those other lay'abouts were even out of their beds!" On realizing what he had just said, the old minister fought to regain his composure, he spoke to himself; "What am I saying? I'm trying to justify the Lords good timekeeping at the wharf." Once he had regained his composure, he sat down again and looked down at Feea who was looking up at him open-mouthed. The old man spoke calmly; "Who told you this piece of nonsense?"

Feea, who wasn't too sure about how his answer might be received, got up and took a step backward, just to make sure that he was out of range and ready to make a quick departure, should the need arise. He spoke as if to console the old man;

"It's true Meenister, a' heard it ma sell jist this morn. Big Murdoch wis shoutin' it 'im." The old minister started to get hot under his clerical collar again: "Big Murdoch! What did Big Murdoch say?"

Feea took another step back before answering. "He said, Jesus Christ, are you late again? Get in ther' an' clean up that damn mess you left yesterday."

The good Reverend was dumfounded and sat open-mouthed as realization descended upon him. He smiled at his own foolishness. 'How silly of me?' He thought to himself shaking his head.

"Of course you wouldn't understand, how could you?"

He got up and put a hand on Feea's shoulder, the little lad cringed.

"Ah Feea, laddie, I don't know what we are going to do with you." Feea spoke hesitantly. "Is it...is it a' richt fur them tae shout at im then?"

The old man spoke reassuringly;

"Well, no, you see, they are taking the Lord's name in vain and that is a sin. I hope you never do that." Feea reassured him with his answer;

"Aw naw, me no see im. Bit if a fine' the vain a'll tak' his name oot an gei it back tae im." He thought for a moment and then asked;

"Whit dis a vain look like? Is it like a boatil?"

The old minister turned away and bit his lip in an effort to stop him from laughing. He looked up to the sky and smiled as he spoke to himself; "Is it like a bottle? Only Feea could ask a question like that." Feea stood, innocently, waiting for an answer but the good Reverend decided that this might be a good time to make a tactful retreat before he gets drawn into another discussion that would tax his nerves and end nowhere. He turned back to Feea and smiled; "Look Feea, don't you fuss yourself about it…. Well, I'll have to be going now." He reached into his pocket and handed Feea a piece of sugar-ally. Feea took it and with a bow, kissed the old man's hand. As always, the old minister was taken aback with the young boy's impeccable manners. He smiled and put his hand on Feea's head and said "God Bless you Feea," then he turned and walked away smiling at the young boy's innocence. Feea stopped eating the sugar-ally and called after the minister;

"A'll look oot fur that vain!"


Feea made his way into Glasgow Green. As he approached the Mollindiner Burn, he saw Curdie lying at the side dangling his feet in the water. "Curdie! Curdie!" he called out as he ran over to the boy. "Look whit av' gote," he showed Curdie the sugar-ally. Curdie's eyes lit up when he saw the treat; "Gonnae gei's a bit," he asked excitedly. Feea duly obliged by breaking the sweet in half and handing the partly chewed half to his friend.

"Where did ye get it?" Curdie asked. "Och, the Meenister gei'd it tae me efter he telt me aboot…. Gee… Gee us Cripes ur sumtin'… ye ken him, thur aye shoutin at him doon at the wharf, they keep is name in a boatil." Curdie looked dumfounded; "Och…. Och aye," he said giving Feea a funny look. They sat by the side of the burn dangling their feet in the water while Feea told Curdie all about his adventures at Craigaven and his trip on the Comet. The heat of the sun made Feea drowsy and he soon fell asleep, dropping his piece of sugar-ally at his side. Curdie, who was anything but slow, snatched it up and was soon chewing away merrily while Feea wandered, barefoot, through the Land of Nod. Curdie's attention was drawn to the boisterous voices of some boys from the Grammar School. They were standing at the Nelson Monument deep in discussion. (The Nelson Monument on Glasgow Green was the first in Great Britain to commemorate the victories of Admiral Lord Nelson).

Robbie, the tallest boy, pointed up at the Monument and addressed the boys; "Whoever throws the ball highest will be the Champion. Now who wants to go first?"

"Let me do it," piped up Hector Jarvis, better known to the boys as 'Titch', due to his small stature. "O.K," said Robbie, handing him the ball.

Titch took the ball and, taking a few paces back, let it fly at the Monument. It went about one third of the way up then fell back to earth.

"Is that it? Is that the best you can do? Let me show you." Robbie picked up the ball and walked back to where 'Titch' had been standing. He drew his arm back as far as he could then he threw the ball with all the force that he could muster. The ball went flying up the column and when it had reached almost two thirds of the way, it fell back towards the ground. There were gasps of "Wow," from the boys as they applauded Robbie's great effort. The rest of the boys tried but could do no better than half way.

Curdie's curiosity got the better of him and he got up and wandered over to the boys, leaving Feea asleep at the side of the burn.

"Whit is it yer dae'n?" he asked as he approached them.

The boys went silent then slowly turned in his direction. Robbie left the group and walked up to Curdie. Haughtily, he looked down at him; "What do you want, beggar boy?" The others came over and gathered round Curdie.

Curdie looked round at the others then addressed Robbie who appeared to be their leader.

"Ah wis jist wunnerin' whit yae wis dae'n, that's aw, ah thoat it wis a gemm."

Robbie looked at the other boys and grinned. He then looked back at Curdie;

"Oh I see, and you would like to play. Is that right?" He said sarcastically.

"Aye that's it, gie's a shote" Curdie answered cheekily.

Robbie looked him straight in the eye;

"Well you can't play because we don't associate with scruffs."

He turned and as he went to join the others Curdie spoke again;

"Och aye, ah see, yer feert ah might beat yae. Is that it?" Robbie stopped in his tracks, then turned and made his way back towards this cheeky little urchin. The others crowded round, menacingly. There were cries of; "Throw the cheeky little beggar in the burn!" Robbie addressed the boys;

"Wait a minute lads, let's be fair. If this little scruff can beat me, then we'll let him go, but if he can't, then in the burn he goes." There were cries of, "YES! YES! As the group got closer, preventing any chance of escape. Curdie looked pathetic as he stood in his rags. With his toes clenched the grass, he looked at the boys; they looked like an army as they stood around him in their pristine school uniforms. He gave them a cheeky grin, more out of nerves than bravery. He followed Robbie over to the Monument. The tall schoolboy handed him the ball; "Lets see what you can do, beggar boy." Curdie took the ball and threw it as hard as he could, but whether it was nerves or bad aiming; the ball went flying passed the monolith to hoots of laughter from the schoolboys. One of the boys recovered the ball and handed it to Robbie. He took aim and threw it about the same height as his last effort. The boys cheered in approval of their champion. Curdie took the ball and tried again. This time the ball went a little over a quarter of the way up. Robbie smirked as the other boys giggled 'Titch' handed him the ball. He threw it again; it went a little higher than his last throw before returning to earth.

No one had noticed Feea who had woken up and wandered over. He stood behind the group of schoolboys watching what was going on. Robbie handed the ball to Curdie; "One more then it's the burn for you, beggar boy." Curdie took the ball and just as he was about to throw it, a voice came from the back; "Me dae it! Me dae it! Me dae it fur Curdie!" The boys went quiet then turned in the direction of the voice. On seeing Feea, they burst into hysterical laughter with cries of, "It's another one and he's even worse than this one." Feea pushed his way through the group of boisterous schoolboys and stood before Robbie; "Oh I see, so you wan't to go in the burn as well?" Robbie said sarcastically. Feea, unaware that the older boy was making a fool of him, answered seriously, "Naw me will loup a stane ower the big spike fur Curdie." The boys started to mimic Feea as they fell about laughing. Robbie held up his hands to try to quieten them down; "Now hold on boys, I have another challenger and we can have the pleasure of dumping both of them in the burn. Now hold the little one and we'll see how this other one fares." He went to hand Feea the ball but he refused it;

"Naw a'll loup ma 'Lucky Chuckie' ower the big spike."

"Your Lucky Chuckie, what's that?" Robbie looked mystified as Feea took a smooth, almost spherical, stone from his pocket; it was almost as big as his hand. He handed it to Robbie who weighed it in his hand. On realizing how heavy it was, he handed it back to Feea; "If you can reach half way with that thing you and your friend can go free; the grin on his face betrayed the fact that he wasn't being charitable with his offer. Robbie was convinced that Feea had no chance of reaching half way up the Monument with such a heavy object. Feea on the other hand was totally convinced that he could do much better and was about to prove it. Feea rubbed the stone on his sleeve then drew his arm back as far as he could. The boys were giggling and laughing as he let it fly. Their laughing faded into silence as the stone climbed higher and higher. The higher it went, the wider their mouths gaped. They couldn't believe their eyes as it went right over the top. Feea ran round to the other side and caught it as it came plummeting to the ground. The boys broke into rapturous clapping and cheering with cries of, "Well done, well done, wee scruffy is the Champion." "Naw me is Feea", the little lad protested.

Excitedly, they gathered round their new, if not unlikely, hero.

Robbie came over and offered his hand to Feea; "Well done, Feea you're a worthy Champion." Feea went to kiss his hand but Robbie stopped him and shook his instead while the other boys rushed forward to clap him on the back. From that day on, Feea became a favourite with the grammar school boys and when they met him, he would be included in their games. He soon became the champion at a game called 'High Spy', which was a form of 'Hide and Go Seek'.

Running was his forte and in this he excelled, for in his bare feet, none of the boys could keep up with him at any distance, and even Robbie, the grammar school champion, was no match for him. Robbie had a great respect for Feea's ability and from then on would always try to get him on his side when they were playing; together; they made a formidable team.

## Captain Mitchell

There was a chill wind blowing as Feea went on the search for food. He decided
to look in a pile of rubbish at the back of a house in Charlotte Street.

Something caught his eye, it was a broken bottle but to Feea's mind it could be a
'vain' like the one that the old minister had been talking about the previous
week and maybe the very one that 'The Lord's Name' had been taken away in.
Feea was so busy examining the inside of the bottle that he didn't notice that he
was being watched from a top window. The observer was Captain Mitchell the
Commissioner of Police and this was his back garden. Mitchell had no love for
children and particularly despised the urchins who roamed the streets and alleys.
Feea turned the bottle upside down and gave it a shake but all that came out was
some dirt that had been stuck at the bottom. He was so intent in what he was
doing that he didn't hear the man creeping up behind him brandishing a riding
crop.

"AND WHAT DO YOU THINK YOU ARE DOING!" Mitchell said in a loud,
authoritarian voice. Feea was startled and dropped the bottle. He turned and
timidly looked up the man towering above him and holding the whip high above
his head.

"Me is jist lookin' fur the vai…" He didn't get time to finish as Mitchell brought
the whip swishing down on the little boy's shoulder. Feea dived through his
assailant's legs in a bid to escape but in his haste, he tripped and bumped his
knee on the ground. He crouched down beside the garden wall. Mitchell
pursued him and started a frenzied attack on the defenceless boy. He lashed and
slashed at him as Feea cowered into the wall. "Me no dae it again!

Me no dae it again!" Feea screamed as the implement of torture cut into his skin
and taking his breath away with every stroke.

Mitchell was shouting as he continued his merciless onslaught;

"This will teach scum like you to stay in the gutter where you belong and not to come near the houses of your betters; I ought to kill you for bringing your verminous body onto my property!"

"No kull Feea! No kull Feea!" The little boy begged.

Mitchell ignored him and continued the assault.

All the screaming and shouting had attracted the attention of William Gilmour, a law student who was on his way to the College in the High Street. He was a tall athletic young man who had won the admiration of his fellow students and was a 'prize' in the opinion of most young ladies. He abhorred injustice and cruelty in any shape or form.

He came from a very 'well to do' family that had two judges and four solicitors in its lineage. His father was a respected lawyer in the city while his uncle Edward held high office in the Privy Council. William was a keen student and hoped, some day, to emulate his father.

He ran into the garden and, grabbing the whip from Mitchell, threw it over the garden wall. Mitchell, who was totally taken by surprise, stood wide-eyed and open-mouthed as the young man unleashed a verbal attack on him. An intense argument ensued.

Gilmour pointed down at Feea crouching against the wall;

"This is outrageous," he said as he looked down at Feea, then he looked straight at Mitchell,

"OUTRAGEOUS!" He shouted right into his face.

The Police Commissioner was fuming, as he had never been spoken to like that before. He gritted his teeth and spoke slowly and deliberately as he stared straight into the young student's eyes;

"Do you 'know' who you are speaking to?"

Gilmour prodded Mitchell in the chest;

"I know 'what' I am speaking to...A Heartless Fiend..."

Mitchell puffed himself up and stood with legs apart as if to show his authority;

"I would like you to know that I am The Commissioner of Police," he pointed his finger, menacingly at the law student, then continued,

"And I would advise you to show some respect."

Gilmour, who wasn't easily intimidated, had an answer for him;

"I reserve my respect for those who deserve it and not for low life miscreants like you." The Police Commissioner looked like he was about to explode;

"Miscreant!!!..... Miscreant!!!..... I think you should keep that description for your resurrectionist friends up in the college...don't you? Maybe your finger nails are caked with grave dirt like your grave-robbing friends." Young Gilmour shook his head slowly and with a sigh spoke with a degree of disgust in his voice;

"You are despicable and a disgrace to your office. If I can find a way in law, I will have you removed from it and ran out of town for the scoundrel that you are."

During the argument, Feea had crawled behind his protector and was holding on to the back of his leg as the heated exchange continued. Mitchell spoke through gritted teeth;

"The only person who is going to be removed is you," he pointed down at Feea, "Now get off my property and take that piece of vermin with you!"

Young Gilmour spoke slowly and looked straight into Mitchell's half crazy eyes;

"It saddens me to think that any adult would describe a child as 'vermin'. Your words and actions are a testament to your character. I pity you 'Mister Commissioner' but I leave you with this promise. I will see to it that long after you and I have departed this life, even when your bones are rotting in the grave, even then, this episode will be remembered. And you, 'Mister Commissioner,' you will be used as an example of all that is cruel and evil in an unjust society."

Mitchell glowered at the young student;

"You upstart! How dare you threaten me! What's your name?"

Young Gilmour helped Feea to his feet;

"Come on child, this is no place for us." He turned and addressed Mitchell; "My name is William Gilmour."

The Police Commissioner spoke with menace in his voice;

"Well, 'Mister Gilmour', be careful how you tread on the streets of Glasgow and have a care that I don't find you with grave dirt in your finger nails. We will meet again, I'll see to it." With that, he made his way back to the house as William helped Feea on their way out of the garden. Feea kept looking back; just to make sure that his assailant wasn't following.

When they were safely outside, William looked down at Feea and was shocked at the state that the little boy was in. "Are you all right," he asked with concern. Feea straightened up and twisted his shoulders from side to side, he looked up at his savoir; "Och me is awe richt noo," he pointed back towards the house; "That man in ther'…him wiz gonnae kull Feea …him wiz gonnae kull Feea awe richt."

With that, he took William's hand and kissed it, then after giving a little bow, ran off towards Glasgow Green, William watched him go. With a shake of his head and a smile of admiration on his face, he turned, and made his way towards the High Street.

## THE OLD GRAVEYARD.

The three boys were standing outside the Old cemetery as Feea and Curdie approached. Unlike the two urchins, the schoolboys had to slip out of their houses undetected. It was a cold night. A brisk wind had got up and was blowing along the deserted street as the bell in the Tollbooth struck midnight. The moon waxed and waned as the clouds drifted across its face and somewhere in the centre of town a dog was barking, while, in a back court was heard an intermittent feline mating call that sounded more like a child in pain.

The three boys were Robbie Munro, Billy 'Titch' Morrison and Robert 'Bogey' MacCallum. 'Bogey' was a fat boy who had earned his nickname because of the obnoxious habit he had of picking his nose at every opportunity. The boys were in boisterous spirits as they went to greet their two bare-footed friends who were scantily dressed in rags while the others were well wrapped up against the elements.

The small group made their way over to the cemetery gates nervously and stood looking in at the eerie scene. Robbie was first to speak.

"We'll draw straws to see who goes first." He bent down and pulled up some blades of grass, then having turned his back to the others, set the blades out in his clenched fist.

"Right," he said, turning back to his friends, "Who ever draws the shortest straw goes first then it's the turn of the next shortest and so forth." The boys nodded in agreement. The task was to see who would go into the graveyard alone and not only go farthest but also stay the longest. It was a boyish game to find out who was the bravest of the group. Each boy picked a blade and then compared them. Curdie had picked the shortest one, and, with a nervous smile and a feeling of foreboding, went over to the gate. He stood there, looking inside at the lines of silent tombstones and hoping that they weren't concealing anything of a ghostly nature.

With a clank and a screech, he pulled back the bolt and pushed the rusty gate open. The others gathered round egging him on.

Curdie was thinking that, maybe this wasn't such a good idea after all. His mind was in serious debated as to the 'pros and cons' of being brave and facing the unknown, or being a coward and leaving someone else to face it. At that point in time, the latter seemed to be the more attractive option.

"Come on, what's keeping you?" Curdie's thoughts were interrupted by the taunts of his companions as they as they grew impatient with his sudden hesitation at the gate.

"Aw richt.Aw richt. A'm gawn," he replied with more than a hint of trepidation in his voice. He entered the cemetery and gingerly walked up the path nervously looking from side to side.

A breeze caused the uncut grass to sway in waves, as if a giant, invisible hand was gently stroking it. This didn't go unobserved by the little lad; whose heart was beating faster with every step that he took. He kept looking back just to make sure that the others were still there; this gave him a little courage as he ventured into the unknown. He followed the path as it went round a bend with bushes on either side. He had only gone a few paces when a gust of wind caused the bushes to shake violently while at that very moment the moon went behind a cloud. Curdie stopped dead in his tracks as if frozen to the spot. He could feel his heart pounding in his chest as every sinew in his body became taught and his senses became alert to every sound and movement around him. His attention was suddenly drawn to a stirring high up in the bush opposite, then without warning, an owl took off, swaying and screeching as it flew overhead. That was it, the straw that not only broke the camel's back, but broke Curdie's nerve as well. Panic took over as he turned and ran back towards the gate shouting and screaming like a scalded cat.

"Thur's a ghost in ther'! Thur's a ghost, a'm no kiddin', a saw it!" He gasped while fighting for breath. The boys laughed and mocked him as he tried, unsuccessfully, to convince them.

"Thur's nae ghosties," Feea said, shaking his head and smiling.

"Thur is, ah saw it. It flew oot o' the bushes. It wis screamin' an tryin' tae get me. If yae don't believe me, come an' see fur yersels" Curdie said in exasperation. This only made things worse with the boys laughing and mimicking the actions of a ghost as they moved around and pretended to scare him. Curdie pushed them away and went back into the cemetery;

"Come oan an' see fur yesel's; if yer no' too feert that is." Curdie's challenge soon calmed them down. Robbie followed him in, then turned to the others;

"Come on then, let's go and see this ghost," he said with a restrained giggle. The boys followed Curdie as he led them to the spot where the owl had sent him into such a panic. The moon came from behind a cloud as the boys stood in the eerie silence. The wind had ceased and the tombstones stood like dwarfed soldiers in the deep grass.

"Well where's the gho…" Robbie didn't get time to finish as the sound of a snapping twig in the bushes right behind them brought their attention into full focus. They turned and to their horror, the bush started moving with the sound of creaking branches and crunching twigs; someone or something was coming out of the bushes towards them. The boys scattered in all directions, running as fast as their legs could carry them. Feea and Curdie ran passed the bushes and dodged between the tombstones with the sound of heavy footsteps right behind them. In unison, they jumped the smaller gravestones like two young stags.

Before them, they saw a large oblong headstone with an eerie glow coming from behind it. On realizing that he wouldn't be able to jump it, Curdie turned and ran down the path. Feea on the other hand was going so fast that he couldn't stop and with a mighty leap, jumped over the top and landed right in the arms of a corpse being dragged from an open grave. Before he had time to recover, two burley mud covered hands, pinned him to the ground. He looked up to see the face of Malky Monachan glowering down at him. Monachan reached over and grabbing a spade was about to decapitate the little lad when another man appeared.

"Hod it Malky! Hod it! He's worth mer tae us if he's hale. Smother the wee brat an' maybe wu'll get six guineas fur him an' the auld bitch thegither."

"Good thinkin' Weasel, good thinkin." The big man growled. The brute dropped the spade and put his filthy hand over Feea's nose and mouth in an attempt to smother him. Feea fought for breath as his assailant pressed harder, cutting off his supply of air. In desperation, Feea reached out and grabbing a handful of dirt; threw it in Malky's face. Instinctively the big man let go and rubbed his stinging eyes.

Feea struggled clear and was off like a shot before Malky had time to recover. In a matter of seconds the two grave robbers were in hot pursuit. The Weasel dived and almost caught the boy's ankle as he dodged behind a wooden cross and made off towards the cemetery wall with the two villains right behind. Without so much as a pause, he leapt right over the wall and disappeared down an alley opposite. His two pursuers were exhausted when they reached wall and leant against it gasping for breath. They looked out into the deserted street.

"How could yae let him get away," gasped the Weasel

"He threw dirt in ma' face, A couldnae see, an' onywei the wee buggar is like an eel, ye cannae hod him." Malky answered in total frustration.

"Well wan thing's fur sure; if he opens his mooth we'll baith swing. So we better get him an' mak damned sure thit he disn'ae talk; it's that wee daft boye, Feea. Efter we get rid a' the auld bitch we'll go searchin' his haunts."

They turned and made their way back to the open grave muttering to each other and cursing their bad luck.

Meanwhile, Feea ran into the Saltmarket and turned into the street that led to McGurk's stable. He heard Scruff's playful yelping as the dog ran up the street to greet him. He ran round the side of the wooden framed building and pushed aside the plank that was his secret entrance. Once he and Scruff were safely inside, he replaced the plank. The little dog was jumping up and yelping as it excitedly greeted its master. Feea crouched down and held the dog to his chest; "Shush! Me is hide'n fae the bad mannies." He whispered and held the dog tightly. Feea and Scruff went over to a corner at the far end of the stable and sat down on the straw. They sat quietly listening for any sounds outside but all they could hear was the sound of the horses' hooves striking the cobbles as they moved restlessly, in their stalls. Feea went over and looked through a crack in the wooden wall, to check that all was clear outside, and then he went back over to the corner where he and Scruff sat and listened for any telltale sound that might warn them of the approaching grave robbers but all was silent outside, so they settled down and after a while fell asleep.

## THE OLD WAREHOUSE

The wind had got up and was causing the unsecured wooden gate out in the yard to swing on its hinges. There was a strong gust that sent it crashing against the wall. Feea jumped up, and thinking that he had been discovered, ran over to the secret entrance and quickly went through, followed by Scruff. They ran down the street and made their way to the wharf were Feea hoped to find sanctuary in the old abandoned warehouse where there would be plenty of places to hide. They ran along the dark deserted streets, stopping every now and then to make sure that they weren't being followed. Scruff was having a great time while Feea was straining his eyes and ears to every noise and movement. When they arrived at the wharf, they turned a corner and there at the top of the street stood the old abandoned warehouse. It looked foreboding, standing, as it did, like a dark satanic cathedral, silhouetted against the moonlit sky.

Feea ran towards it with Scruff close behind.

A tall wooden door hung off its hinges, almost blocking the entrance to the derelict building. Feea stopped beside it and looked back down the street to make sure that he wasn't being observed before entering the crumbling building. Scruff was right at his heels when he squeezed his way past the door that was hanging at a very precarious angle.

The inside of the building was a chaotic shambles with wooden beams, twisted floorboards and broken masonry lying all over the place. The upper floors had collapsed when part of the roof had fallen in, leaving the interior exposed to the elements. The wooden floor was rotten and damp and the whole place was stinking with the smell of decomposing wood and vegetation. A yellowish mist lay like a carpet across the floor giving the place an atmosphere of total dereliction. The whole structure was fraught with danger. The floorboards squeaked as Feea made his way across them. Scruff held back sensing some kind of danger. Feea had almost reached the other side when there was a loud creak followed by an even louder 'SNAP' as part of the floor collapsed sending him hurtling down into the cellar, amidst cascading timber and masonry. He landed unconscious, on the stone floor surrounded by the fallen debris.

With all the commotion, Scruff had run back to the door and was standing with an inquiring look on his face as he looked over at the hole in the floor. Dust billowed from the opening and settled on the beams that were sticking out at all angles from its depths.

Silence, like the dust, settled on the scene as moonbeams filtered through the opening in the roof, everything was still, it was as if a silent sound had filled the place, like the 'hiss' you get in your ears in the middle of the night when everything is quiet. The little dog got down on its tummy and started to crawl towards the gaping hole. It looked over the edge at the scene of devastation below.

Feea was lying, sprawled out on the floor with his hair partly covering his face. A small pool of blood had formed near his forehead where he had been struck by some falling debris. He was lying perfectly still as the little dog's attention was drawn to a movement in the shadows over by the cellar wall. A little pair of red eyes was staring out from the gloom, soon another pair then another and another joined them. Scruff got agitated as more and more of them appeared and was soon followed by a crescendo of hideous squeaking. It was a nest of rats that had been disturbed by the falling debris, now they were coming to investigate the scene. They moved towards the unconscious Feea with their little noses and whiskers twitching as they moved their heads from side to side sniffing the air. The ravenous creatures had detected the scent of blood and were moving in to gorge themselves.

Scruff jumped up and started pacing backward and forwards along the edge of the hole, while keeping his eyes on the vile little rodents below. He started yelping and growling, as they got closer to his friend. The rats ignored him and continued towards their helpless prey. The little dog became frantic when the first rat started sniffing at Feea's hand while the rest surrounded him. He ran round to where the beams were sticking out of the hole, and without hesitation, jumped onto the first beam and slithered down into the midst of the rats, snarling, growling and biting every one of the creatures that were within striking distance. He ran at the ones that were trying to escape and jumped on them tearing at their necks in a frenzied onslaught. The rats scattered in all directions leaving a dozen or more of their companions lying dead on the cellar floor. Scruff paraded along the cellar walls looking for any stragglers that might be lurking about. When he was satisfied that there were none, he climbed onto Feea's back and kept watch over his friend. He started to lick Feea's face in an effort to waken him and finding that there was no reaction, started to yelp. The little dog lay across Feea's back and began to whine. Its pathetic cries travelled up from the cellar and out into the cold night air.

Jean Muldoon and Tommy Watson were standing in a back close halfway down the street. Tommy was getting a bit amorous while Jean was having none of it.

"If ye paw ma breest wan mair time a'll knee ye where it hurts." There was frustration in Jean's voice as she took Tommy's hand and for the third time, placed it back round her neck. She was a tall, buxom girl in her early twenties with flaming red hair and a mind of her own. Being the daughter of an innkeeper, she was well used to dealing with awkward situations. Tommy, not being used to not getting his own way, sighed and accepted the rejection.

"Och Jean, ye dinna ken whit it dis tae me when a'm stawn'n' sae close tae a braw lass like yer sel', ah mean, a' wan't tae touch her, a'canna help ma'sell."

"Try!" was Jean's curt reply, and she meant it. Tommy tried pleading;

"Bit ye dinna ken whit it dis tae me lass,"

"A' ken weel enough whit it did tae Effie Macintosh." Tommy capitulated;

"That wis a bit below the belt."

"Aye, in mair wies than wan." Jean replied with a smirk.

"Yer an awfae lass Jean Muldoon." Tommy said, shaking his head. They went into an embrace. Just as Tommy was about to let his hand slip down to the forbidden territory, a plaintiff whine was heard. Jean pushed Tommy away;

"Whit wis that?" She said, holding him at bay while she listened. It had stopped and all was silent again.

"A' didnae hear onythin'. Whit wis it?" Tommy asked being annoyed at the interruption to his advances.

"A' don't know, it sounded like a dug in pain." Jean had no sooner spoken than the whining started again.

"There it is, kin ye hear it?" They went to the close mouth and looked up the street as the whining continued.

"A' think its cummin' fae the auld warehouse," Jean concluded.

Tommy, being an animal lover and having a dog of his own, decided to investigate, just in case there was a dog trapped in the derelict building. Jean followed him as he made his way towards the, now, moonlit ruin. When they arrived at the entrance, Tommy popped his head inside then withdrew.

"It looks awfae dangerous in ther'. You stiye oot here while a' go in an' see if a' kin fin' the dug." Jean nodded and stood at the side of the slanted door while Tommy squeezed past it and entered the building. He could hear the whining coming from the hole in the floor. He went to cross over but drew back when he heard a creak and felt the floor dip. The whole thing felt unstable. Sticking close to the wall, he made his way round to the gaping hole in the floor. Standing with his back against the wall, he peered down into the cellar. When his eyes were accustomed to the dark, he saw Scruff, who was now standing beside Feea and yelping his head off. He realized that the little boy, if not badly hurt, was certainly in a very dangerous situation. Slowly he made his way back to the door and squeezed his way back outside. Jean quizzed him excitedly; "Did ye find it? Is it aw right?" She enquired.

"It's no' the wee dug thit's in trouble, it's that wee beggar boye, ye know, the wan they call Feea. It looks like he fell through the fler. Ah' think he's badly hurt, if no' deid. We'll need tae get some help." There was real concern in Tommy's voice.

"Come oan we'll get ma da, he'll ken whit tae dae." Jean said, pulling on Tommy's sleeve as she ushered him away.


When they arrived at the Inn, Paddy Muldoon was clearing up and trying to get the place back into some semblance of order after a busy night. Jean hurried over to her father;

"Da' Ye'll need tae come an' help us. Wee Feea's fell through the fler in the auld warehoose an' Tommy thinks thit he might be deid." Paddy stopped what he was doing and glanced over at Tommy with a look of fatherly concern; "An' whit would you two be do'n up at the auld warehoose then?" Jean butted in on her father's prying question before Tommy had time to answer; "Oh, we were jist passin' when we heard wee Feea's dug whinin' in the auld buildin'. Tommy went in an' found the wee boye lyin' in the cellar." Knowing Tommy's reputation, Paddy wasn't convinced but realizing that there was more important work at hand, he let it go and ran into the room behind the bar. He came back carrying a rope and a lantern.

"Come on now, we'd better be hurry'n," he said as he quickly made his way out the door with Jean and Tommy right behind him.

When they got to the warehouse, Paddy, being the strapping Irish man that he was, put the rope and lantern down before taking grip of the door and, pulling it off its remaining hinge and sent it clattering to the ground. Tommy took the lantern and entered the building with the Irishman following on carrying the rope.

"I'll show you where he is but you'll hiv' tae keep close tae the wa', the hale fler is ready tae cave in. A'll lead the wei." Paddy nodded in agreement. With Jean waiting outside, they made their way round to the opening in the floor where Scruff was yelping his head off. Tommy held the lantern over the opening;

"Look ther' he is, ah think he's in a bad wei," He said as Paddy looked down into the cellar. Paddy looked at the situation for a few minutes then made a decision.

"Well you jist be getting' yourself down one of those beams an' a'll be lowerin' the rope to you. Then you'll be tie'n it round the wee lad so thit a' kin pull him up, bit watch yersell, a' don't trust this fler at all." Although the opening was only four feet from the wall, to Tommy it felt like forty as he stepped on to its creaking surface with a feeling of trepidation and impending doom. He put the lantern down and reaching out, grabbed one of the beams that were sticking up and swung his body on to it. Gingerly, he started his descent into the cellar. Scruff became more excited, the closer Tommy got to the cellar floor. He was running backward and forward with his little tail swishing from side to side and stopping every now and then to give a few yelps as if he was saying, "Hurry up and rescue us!"

Tommy stepped off the beam with the little dog, excitedly, jumping up and down at his heels. He crossed over to where Feea was lying and bent down to examine him. Then he shouted back up through the hole;

"He's still alive, bit a' think he his banged his heed oan somethin!"

"Awe right, then a'll toss the rope doon. Tie it round his waist an' get him over to the beam. Then while I'll be pulling him up, you'll be steadying him." Paddy had no sooner finished speaking than the rope landed beside Tommy's feet, scaring the life out of Scruff. Tommy quickly tied it round the unconscious boy and lifted him over to the beam. He called up for Paddy to take the strain as he helped by pushing Feea up the beam. The floor was creaking alarmingly as Paddy pulled on the rope. Tommy was climbing the beam while supporting Feea on his shoulders. When Paddy saw the little lad's head and shoulders appear at the top, he put one foot on the floor and jerked Feea clear of the hole. He then pulled him towards the comparative safety of the wall where he took the rope off and keeping close to the side, carried the unconscious boy towards the door while Tommy went back down to get Scruff. The young man scooped the little dog up and held it under his arm as he negotiated climbing the beam with one hand. After slipping back a few times he eventually reached the top and released the dog.

Scruff ran over to the door as Tommy climbed out of the hole.

Just as he was about to cross to the wall, there was a series of creaks as the floor started to sag and groan.

Without hesitation, he turned, ran across the sinking floor and dived through the door just as the floor buckled and disappeared with a deafening crash, into the cellar behind him. He landed in a heap beside Jean, who had almost jumped out of her skin when he came flying out of the doorway. Tommy picked himself up and rubbed his leg that he twisted when he landed awkwardly.

"Phew! That wis close," he exclaimed with a long drawn out sigh.

"Where is yer da' an' Feea?" He asked, looking around.

"Ma da's kerried him doon tae the Inn. We've tae get doon ther' as quick as we kin. The wee dug went tearin' away efter them. Ur ye aw right?" Jean asked as she watched Tommy rubbing his leg.

"Aye am fine," he replied, "a' jist banged ma leg when a' fell. Come oan we better get doon ther' an' see how the wee boye is."

When they arrived at the inn Paddy was using a wet cloth to clean the dirt and grime off Feea's forehead.

"How is he?" Tommy enquired.

"Och now, sure he'll be foin; he's just taken a knock." Paddy said, wiping a streak of dried blood from the side of the little boy's face.

Feea opened his eyes and putting a hand to his head, grimaced.

"Ouch," he uttered, rubbing a swelling near the crown. "Me's gote a lump oan ma heed an' its sare."

Scruff, who was sitting near him, started to lick his face. Feea sat up and pushed him away.

"No' dae that, dug, me no' like it," he said but the little dog was insistent, and, with its tail wagging, excitedly, jumped up onto his lap and started again. Feea lifted Scruff down onto the floor and hesitantly, got to his feet. Paddy grabbed him as he staggered and almost fell over.

"Oi t'ink ye'd better sit down 'til ye find yer sea legs," he said with a grin and helped him over to a seat. The innkeeper turned to his daughter. "Jean me darlin', go and fetch some water for the lad."

The girl went through to the back of the inn and returned with a beaker. She handed it to Feea who gulped the liquid down.

"Not so fast," Paddy said, putting his hand on Feea's to stop him from gulping the water. "Just sip it lad." Feea did as he said while glancing sideways at his surroundings.

"Whit's this place?" he asked with a glazed look in his eyes.

"Why, its Paddy's Inn, don't you know where ye are? Sure, you've been here on many occasions, you usually sit outside there in the Saltmarket and it's not the

first time that you'd be dancin' for me customers outside the door. Oi'm
t'inking that you must be a little dazed with the fall, 'tis better that you just rest
yourself 'till you feel a little better."

The blank expression on the boy's face showed that the knock on the head had
caused him to loose his memory. He had no idea where he was or who these
people were. He just sat there trying to remember, but his mind was a complete
blank. The events of that night and all that had gone before had been
completely wiped out. Paddy patted him on the shoulder.

"It'll come back to you, now, so don't go gettin' yourself in a state." He turned
to his daughter, "Jean, go and fetch some food for the little lad, he must be
starvin', and bring some ale for me-self and young Tommy here." Feea ate
heartily and slowly but surely, his memory returned, well most of it, it was still a
bit foggy about what made him run into the old warehouse in the first place; he
knew that it had something to do with the graveyard but couldn't remember
what. After a while and after thanking the Muldoons and Tommy, Feea and
Scruff went back to the stables where they settled down for the night. His sleep
was troubled by scenes of him running through the streets being pursued by two
dark strangers. Apart from that he slept soundly with Scruff at his side; they
were oblivious to the dark clouds that were gathering over the old city.

# AGENT PROVOCATEUR

Lightning flashed across a thunderous sky as sheets of torrential rain came crashing down on the coach as it sped through the night. The driver fought with the reins as the terrified horses, with nostrils flaring, bolted on through the storm as they made their way towards the outskirts of Glasgow.

It was two-o'clock in the morning when the coach, finally pulled up outside the Black Bull Inn, which was situated at the far end of the Trongate.

The rain was pelting down as the coachman descended from his waterlogged driving seat. He opened the door of the coach and spoke to the occupant.

"We're here sir; this is the Black Bull Inn."

"Well don't just stand there, knock them up. You don't expect me to do it, do you?" an arrogant English voice retorted from the dark recess of the coach.

With a grunt, the coachman went over and banged on the tavern door, he waited for a moment then banged again; there was no reply. "Do you expect me to sit out here all night?" The agitated Englishman called out. "Bang the door harder. Get the Scottish scoundrels up and be quick about it." He was starting to sound frustrated as he mumbled some obscenities about Scotland, the Scottish people and the Scottish weather, as if they came together as a set just to annoy him.

Scotland didn't look very 'Bonnie' to this insensitive Sassenach.

The coachman pounded on the door with his clenched fist, wishing that it were his passenger that was at the receiving end of his efforts, but, having no such luck, he vented his anger on the door.

"Aw right! Aw, right! " Came a voice from inside. The door opened and the innkeeper stood in his nightgown and cap holding a candle that he shielded with his hand. "Wha ..." but before he had time to speak, the passenger pushed the door open and barged in sweeping the innkeeper aside.

"Whit the hell dae yae think yer dae'n, force'n yer wei in here at this time o' the night? Dae ye think we dinna...", he was stopped in mid sentence by the irate passenger.

"Keep a civil tongue in your head you insolent little maggot and take that hat off your head when you are in my presence," the man interrupted. "I am Sir Percival Barrington. You do have a reservation for me...don't you?" he continued indignantly.

"Och aye, furgie me yer lordship a' didna ken that it wis yersel" the innkeeper grovelled. Grovelling came natural to Fergus when he was in the presence of those of a higher station than his was. This was due to the years that he had spent in service, before an uncle died and left him The Black Bull, which was the best establishment of its kind in Glasgow.

Sir Percival had a foreboding appearance, as he stood there, dressed completely in black. His tall intimidating stature towered over the little innkeeper who had gone white by this time and was visibly shaking, a mixture of fear and cold, no doubt.

The burly coachman entered carrying a large trunk that he set down on the floor. A smaller man carrying cases quickly followed him; he put these beside the trunk. Sir Percival glowered at the innkeeper;

"Get me some claret and make sure that it's your best vintage, and then you can help my servants to carry the luggage up to my room."

He took off his broad-brimmed hat and cloak then sat down at a table near the fire. It still had some glowing embers so Fergus went over and put some more wood on it before hurrying away to fetch the wine.

When he came back the fire was ablaze. He placed a lit candle on the table and poured some wine from a crystal decanter into a broad goblet, he then placed it before his guest. Sir Percival took a sip then turned to the innkeeper.

"Now be off about your business and when my accommodation has been prepared, send Clarence, my manservant, to me."

Haughtily, he dismissed the innkeeper with a hand gesture then sat and sipped his wine while the others struggled upstairs with the luggage.

He sat and pondered on the reason that he had been sent to Glasgow. It grew out of rumours that were circulating in London about unrest among the lower classes in Scotland, especially the weavers and that there was talk of rebellion in Glasgow. His mission, with government backing, was to find out if there was any truth in this and if it was the case then his job was to see that the ringleaders were brought to book by using any means that he saw fit. In the morning, he was to meet a man who would keep him informed about anything that was untoward among the lower classes, a scoundrel by the name of Bob Minto. Minto was the type of character who would sell his own grandmother; actually, he had done just that. After she died, he and two acquaintances, namely, Malky Monachan and The Weasel dug her up and sold her body to the doctors up at the College. Minto walked with a limp, having one leg shorter than the other and having bowlegs as well, tended to make him walk like a chimpanzee with a bunion. He used to have a crutch but lost that in a game of marbles with some school kids, (they could cheat better than he could). They used to play Shinty on Glasgow Green with it while Bob hobbled past, cursing them for all he was worth. They in turn just laughed and made rude gestures in his direction while mimicking his unusual, if not unique, gait. Minto was a character best to be avoided.

"Your room is ready sir," Sir Percival's train of thought was interrupted by the arrival of his manservant, Clarence, who picked up his master's things then led him up to his room.

It was mid-morning when Sir Percival arose and having finished his ablutions was dressing with the aid of Clarence. He had just decided on which shirt to wear when there was a rap on his bedroom door. Clarence stopped what he was doing and went to answer it. On opening the door, he was confronted by Fergus the innkeeper. "There's a man down stairs asking for your master," he said with a note of concern in his voice. "Thank you innkeeper," the servant replied then closed the door and conveyed the information to his master who nodded and continued dressing.

Bob Minto was drinking ale at a table near the window when the innkeeper approached, closely followed by Sir Percival and his servant. "This is the man," the innkeeper announced with a slight bow to the tall Englishman. "Thank you, leave us now, and show my servant to the stables. "Clarence, make sure that Hobson has my coach gleaming," "Yes sir I'll see to it," Clarence replied with a nod. With a wave of his hand, Sir Percival dismissed the two men and turned to the man at the table. "Do you know who I am?" he asked with a stern gaze at the man seated before him.

"Aye a' ken who yae ur aw richt, yer the big wig frae Lundin"

Bob got up and held out his grubby hand: "Ma name is Minto, Bob Minto," Sir Percival ignored the gesture, not wishing to touch the germ-infested thing. He sat down opposite the man and, making sure to avoided the man's fowl smelling breath, began to quiz him;

"Well Minto, what do you have to tell me?"

Minto looked agitated as he glanced around to make sure that they weren't being observed; "Well furst yer Lordship thur's the little matur o' the money." Sir Percival looked shocked;

"How dare you, you vile little creature, how dare you bring my honour into question."

"Weel, fer's fer yur Worship, av' gote whit you wan't an' you've gote whit a wan't. Nae disrispek 'r onythin, its jist the wei a dae business. Onywei ye'll be gled wae whit a've gote fur yae."

Sir Percival reached into his pocket and brought out a golden guinea. With a click, he placed it on the table between himself and Minto. Saliva formed at the side of the little man's mouth as he gazed at the shining coin. He went to grab it but Sir Percival anticipated his move and drew it back.

"Not until you give me something worthy of this," he said, keeping the coin out of Minto's reach.

The little man pursed his lips; "Weel wur baith in luck, fur durin' that storm last nicht, the Nelson Monumunt in the Green gote hit wae the lightnin' an' a big bit gote noked aff the tap. Thur's a fair crowd getherin' roon it an maist o' the wans thit yer lookin fur wull be ther. A'll peint thum oot tae ye an ye kin dae whit ye wan't wae thum, bit a'll want mair thin that if ye wan't me tae get thum riled up fur ye."

Sir Percival looked satisfied and replaced the coin, which was swiftly snatched up by his companion. He got up from the table and looked down at Minto, who was biting the coin:

"If you do a good job there will be two more for you. So be off and I will see you at the Monument." The little man's eyes lit up when he heard this and on rising, rushed out the door.

Sir Percival called over to the innkeeper; "Go and tell my servants to bring my coach round to the front door." He then went upstairs to collect some items that might be needed. These included a small biretta pistol that he carried inside his topcoat when he thought that there might be some element danger.

# THE TRAP IS SPRUNG

The crowd standing around the Monument was getting larger as more people arrived to see the shattered appearance of the monolith. The top had been completely severed by the blast of the lightning bolt. People were pointing up and staring in awe at the immense power that was in Nature. Almost three feet had been blasted from the top and a yawning crack ran all the way to the ground. Feea wandered onto the Green. His attention was drawn to the crowd; he wondered why they were there. As he approached, it soon became apparent and he started to giggle at the state of the great monument. He wandered over and pushed his way through the crowd until he was standing in front of the column. His eyes followed the crack all the way up until it reached the top, some one hundred and forty feet above the ground. He smiled and stepped back a few paces, then he took his well-polished stone from his pocket and started to rub it on the sleeve of his ragged shirt. He kept his eyes on the top of the monolith as if he was mesmerized.

The crowd grew silent as one by one they turned and looked at him, wondering what he was doing. The Weasel and Malky were mingling in the crowd when Malky grabbed his partners arm:

"It's him ...It's him," he said excitedly, almost pulling the sleeve off the Weasel's jacket.

"Awe richt! Awe richt a kin see him. Ya big tumshie ye nearly pult the erm ofe ma jaykit," uttered the Weasel, with more than a hint of frustration in his voice.

"Bit it's him! It's him, it's the wee buggar thit saw us in the Graveyard...OUCH!" The Weasel cut the sentence short with a swift kick that landed on Malky's shin.

"Whit did ye dae that fur?" Malky complained while rubbing his leg. The Weasel pulled on the big man's lapel and spoke into his ear; "Ur yae gonnae shut yer mooth, ur maybe yae wan't tae stawn ower at the monument an announce it tae the World. Wan thing's fur sure, the next time ye saw the monument ye'd be facin' it."

(During a public hanging the prisoner would stand facing East in the direction of the Nelson Monument. This would be the last thing that he saw before the drop)

Sir Percival and his servant were standing at the back of the crowd, observing all that was going on and wondering why the crowd had gone quiet. Then he heard intermittent voices in the crowd; "It's wee Feea…. Whit's he dae'n? Ah think he's gonnae try an' noke the Monument doon wae a stane…" The sound of laughter followed the last comment. Then all attention turned to the little boy rubbing the stone. The voices went silent. It was like the crowd at a Bullfight awaiting the 'coup de grace'.

Feea drew back his arm and then let fly with all his might.

All eyes followed the object as it climbed higher and higher in its ascent of the monolith. It kept going until, with a gasp from the crowd, it went right over the top. Feea ran round to the other side and as the crowd scattered from the descending object, he caught it before it reached the ground. A great cheer went up followed by tumultuous applause as the people realized that they had witnessed a truly great feat. Even Sir Percival had an approving grin on his face.

"Did ye see whit he did, did ye see it," Malky said, pulling at the Weasels sleeve again. Wullie slowly lifted the big man's hand from his arm; "It's no whit he did, it's whit he might dae thit worries me," he said sarcastically. "Come oan we better get efter him," he added on noticing that the little lad had run off down the Green in the direction of the Mollindiner Burn. When he got to it he leapt across to the other side and on stopping, looked back towards the Monument. To his horror, he recognized the two men running towards him and his memory of the previous night came flooding back. Without hesitation, he took off like a hare. Malky was about two yards in front of the Weasel as they approached the burn. "Jump the burn! Jump the burn!" the Weasel shouted as the two men ran towards the edge of the fast flowing stream. At the last minute, Malky's nerves went and he stopped dead in his tracks. The Weasel's momentum sent him, crashing into the big man, sending both men headlong into the icy water. They picked themselves upand climbed out of the water. As they sat dripping wet on the bank of the stream, the Weasel turned to Malky who was sitting with his head in his hands, there was utter frustration in the little man's voice as he addressed his companion;

"Am no gonnae ask why ye did that. Aw a kin say is; your mither has a lot tae answer fur!"

By this time, Feea had made his escape.

He decided to hide in the sheds down at the docks, then, later when it would start to get dark he would make his way back to McGurk's stable with Scruff.

Meanwhile the crowd at the Monument had swollen with the arrival of a group of weavers who were led by a man called Billy Cadzow, a local agitator and man of the people. He was a good man who tried to right the wrongs in an unjust society but justice, in whatever form, has its own rules and will, vehemently, oppose all challengers whether they be good or bad. Billy climbed onto a block of fallen masonry and started to make a speech about the appalling conditions that the weavers were living and working in. He went on about the merchants in London and how they were living in the lap of luxury which was being paid for by the slave labour north of the Border.

There were cries of 'Shame' and 'Disgrace' coming from the crowd.

The mood was getting decidedly angry as Bob Minto approached Sir Percival who was busy making notes in his diary. "They're aw here," he said and then proceeded to give the Englishman a list of all the would-be trouble makers; some of whom were merely people that he didn't like. Sir Percival noted the names down in his little book; on his way to the Green, he had called into the barracks close by and alerted the commanding officer to be ready for trouble in the park. A Company of Dragoons and foot soldiers were positioned to the east of the Monument and just out of sight. They were instructed to wait for a signal from Sir Percival before moving in and surrounding the crowd. One of the soldiers was positioned in a spot so that he could keep an eye on Sir Percival. The signal would be the removal of his hat.

Sir Percival gave two guineas to Minto and told him to go and finish the job. Minto turned and pushed his way into the crowd. Soon his voice could be heard above the rest;

"We're no gonnae stawn fur it ony longer. It's time tae dae somthin aboot they lap dugs in the Toon Hall. They're only in it fur thumsels. Let's get thum oot noo an' tak ower the Toon wursels."

There were cries of "aye let's burn thum oot," from the crowd.

Billy Cadzow tried to gain control and appealed for calm but it was to no avail, Minto had done his job well. The crowd started to surge away from the Monument. Sir Percival gave the signal and with the clatter of hooves, the Dragoons who were swiftly followed by the foot soldiers, with bayonets at the ready, surrounded the crowd. Some of the people managed to escape but most of them were held. Sir Percival went over to the officer in charge and on taking a page from his pocket book, handed it to him; "I want these men charged with insurgence. You can let the rest go. If anyone refuses to give his name or causes any bother what so ever, charge them as well." He then stood back with his servant Clarence by his side while the officer and six soldiers went among the crowd. Soon all the people had been dispersed, except for a small group of fourteen men who were made to sit on the grass with there hands on their heads and encircled by the points of as many bayonets. The officer came over to Sir Percival; "There all here sir but there is one who on speaking to me in private, insists that he was working for you."

"Oh really, bring him over." The officer went back to the group then returned with Bob Minto hobbling between two burly soldiers.

"Well done," Sir Percival exclaimed, "that's the one who stole three guineas from my person. I'm sure that if you look in his pocket, you will find them." One of the soldiers went through Minto's pockets and produced the coins.

"Splendid," Sir Percival smirked, "Now you can charge him with theft as well. Take him back to the rest of the scoundrels."

Minto was unceremoniously, dragged back to the others, amidst a tirade of obscenities that were directed at Sir Percival's lineage and homeland. If Minto's compatriots were to find out what treachery he had been up to, he wouldn't have lasted the night with them; the traitor had been betrayed and there was nothing that he could do about it.

With a satisfied grin on his face, Sir Percival made his way back to his coach, and was off, back to the inn, well contented with his day's work. The following morning he would face the conspirators in open court and give a personal account of that day's activities. His word would carry great sway with the judge and there would be no doubt that the prisoners would be convicted and sentenced. Then he would be off, back over the Border and on to London, back to what, to his pompous mind, he classed as 'civilization' when, in fact, the conditions in London were no better and in some ways, much worse than those in Glasgow. However, as his estate was outside the Capital and he didn't have occasion to visit its less attractive quarters, it was home and to him it was 'civilized'.


Malky and The Weasel dried themselves at a workman's brazier on the edge of the Green, and then they made their way along the Gallowgate.

"We'll hiv tae find oot where that wee brat bides, then we kin tak care o' him," The Weasel said through gritted teeth. Malky nodded in agreement. As they approached the Cross, The Weasel noticed some boys sitting on a pile of crates; one of the boys was Curdie, he walked over to them.

"Dae ye ken the wee boye Feea," he asked.

"Aye we ken him," they all answered in unison.

"Dae ye ken whor he bides," The Weasel enquired.

"Och aw ower the place," one of the boys quipped.

"He sleeps in that stable doon near the Green, ye ken the wan, McGurks, the wan wae the widden gates," Curdie said.

"Wit dae ye wa'nt him fur?" Another boy asked.

"Och nuthin', A wis jist wunnerin' where he wis biedin'," The Weasel answered and then went back to Malky.

"We'll get him the nicht" he growled, making a gesture with his finger across his throat: Malky nodded. They continued along the street and went into The Saracen's Head Tavern where they sat down to make plans for that evening's dastardly escapade.


When the men had left the boys looked at eachother and began to worry for Feea's safety.


"Whit dae yea think they wa'nt him fur?" one of them asked.

"A shouldnae hiv telt them", Curdie said, holding his forehead in his hand.

"A think they're gonnae herm him" another boy quipped.

"We'd bet'er go an' warn him", another boy added.

They all agreed and went looking for Feea. They looked in McGurk's stable then went searching the alleys, backcloses and the Green but couldn't find him. They saw Paddy Muldoon sweeping the entrance to his pub and ran up to him telling him their fears for the safety of Feea.

Malky went inside and approached Wullie Balornock who was sitting at a table drinking some ale.

On hearing what Paddy had told him, Willie got up from the table and after swallowing the last of his ale; turned to Paddy.

"A'll go an' get Jock an' we'll look for him", and with that he disappeard out the door.

Paddy told his other customers and they set out to look for Feea, but to no avail so they gave up for the night when it got dark. They would continue their search the next day.

## SHADOW OF EVIL

The wind was howling through the old town causing the litter to go flying in all directions. Windows were rattling and doors banging as it gusted round corners and extinguishing most of the oil lamps in the streets. It was a wild night with a wind that blew with a fury that would take your breath away; a night when the bloodshot eyes of death peered, menacingly, from the shadows.

Old Tam Bryson left the warmth of his fire, and with a degree of unsteadiness in his gait, crossed over to a window that was rattling so much he thought it was going to come in at any minute. He stuffed a piece of rag between the sash and frame as rain started to lash the window; this stopped the rattling. He peered down into the dark street just in time to see a wooden crate crashing against the wall of the tenement opposite; but, with his fading eyesight, he failed to see the two dark figures skulking in the gloom near the end of the lane. "Whit a nicht," he mumbled, shaking his head. With trembling hands, he took hold of a pair of shabby curtains and drew them together then he shuffled back to the warmth of the fireside. He lit his old clay pipe and sat back in his chair. A puff of smoke from the bowl of his pipe slowly drifted towards the ceiling as he listened to the roaring sound that was coming down the flue as the wind gusted passed the chimney pots high up on the roof.

Meanwhile, down in the darkness and beyond earshot, a whispered conversation was taking place in the lane.

"So its McGurk's stable thit he's bidein' in. Well, we'll hiv' tae be quick an' get him while this racket's gawn oan. A'll stick him while you tak' care o' that wee mongrel o' his." The weasel gently played with the point of his dagger as he spoke. "Aye," Mungo answered, giving The Weasel an understanding nudge that almost caused the smaller man to stab his finger. The Weasel let out an exasperate sigh. (At that moment a thought flashed through his mind that maybe it would be better to stick big Malky and take his chances with Feea); but it soon passed. He gripped the big man's arm and with his left eye nervously twitching, stared at him with a look of pure evil, "Come oan let's get it done, while a still hiv a' ma fingers," he said through gritted teeth.

The two men made their way through the shadows while the storm raged around them. The howling wind blew into their faces, almost lifting them off their feet while sheets of torrential rain lashed down from the heavens and soaked them to the skin; it was as if the elements were trying to stop these two ogres in their diabolical quest.

They arrived at the gates to the stable yard just as a flash of lightning lit up the sky and was quickly followed by a clap of thunder. Using all his strength, Malky pulled and hauled on the gates until the wooden slat that was holding the chain snapped.

The two men entered the yard and stealthily made their way over to the stable door. Inside Feea was fast asleep on the straw in the corner. Scruff, who was at his side, woke up and, with ears pricked, stared at the door and growled.

All of a sudden the door burst open and there standing in silhouette against a thunderous sky were the two fiends. Feea woke with a start as Scruff ran towards the men, growling and snapping at their feet. Malky drew his foot back and with one hefty kick lifted the little dog right off the ground and sent it crashing against the wall.

Scruff let out a loud yelp then fell to the cobbled floor and lay motionless. Feea ran over shouting the little dog's name but as he passed The Weasel, he felt a thud and a deep pain in his back. He ignored the pain and bent down, picked up

Scruff and rushed with him in his arms towards the secret entrance. Just as he was about to go through, The Weasel raised his dagger and was about to stab him again, when Bella, the Clydesdale, burst out of her stall neighing and kicking out in all directions; one of her kicks knocked the dagger out of The Weasel's hand and sent it skimming across the stable floor. The two assailants turned on their heels and ran for their lives back out the door. Feea dived through the hole in the wall and ran, crying, down the side street towards the Green; holding the little dog's lifeless body tight in his arms. Lightning flashed across the sky as the rain pelted down. As he entered the park, he slipped and went crashing down onto the wet grass where he lay panting for air. Then he picked himself up and ran, swaying and stumbling, into the bushes. He sat down at the base of a tree and with the body of his little dog on his lap, buried his head in his hands and sobbed inconsolably. All around him, the lashing rain and peels of thunder drowned out the pathetic sound of the young boy sobbing in the undergrowth.

# GOING HOME

Next morning, Wullie and Jock searched the lanes and backcourts while Jamie, Jean and Curdie searched the Green. The two policemen were searching Feea's haunts and hideouts when they entered McGurk's stable. Being Sunday morning, there was no one about. They wondered why the gate to the stable yard was lying open. Wullie searched the yard while Jock went inside the stables. The tall policeman was moving some boxes when Jock came rushing to his side;

"Ye'd better come and hiv a look at this," he said breathlessly. Wullie followed him into the stable. Jock led the way over to a corner of the dimly lit building. The horses seemed to be agitated as they moved around in their stalls and Wullie noticed that one of them had broken free. The old Clydesdale was standing eating some hay at the far wall, totally oblivious of the two intruders. There were signs of a struggle in the corner with straw scattered across the floor and what appeared to be a blood trail leading to a loose board on the wall. Jock bent down and picked up an object; he showed it to Wullie; "What dae ye think o' this?" He said handing it to his partner. Wullie examined it and recognized it as the stiletto dagger that the Weasel had dropped in the tavern; only this time it had blood on it.

"Borland and Monachan hiv been here. This is Borland's knife. He drapped it in Muldoon's tavern when ah broke up a fight there the ither night. We'd better get them before they find Feea. It looks like the wee man's been injured," he said, handing the knife back to Jock.

The two men went outside and examined the loose board at the side of the stable. Jock pointed to the ground; "This must be how the wee lad made his escape. Look there's some spots o' blood leadin' doon the street."

They followed the trail but, with the previous night's rain, lost it near the Green.

Jock decided that they should search near the old wooden bridge that crossed the Clyde. They searched all day, but to no avail.

Meanwhile, the others had split up. Jamie and Curdie were searching along the riverside while Jean looked along the paths leading to the Monument. She could hear the others calling Feea's name as she checked the bushes on either side of the path leading back towards the town. Jean had gone about half way when she heard a moan in the undergrowth. She made her way in and found Feea sitting propped up against a tree with Scruff on his lap, it was obvious that the little dog was dead. Jean called out to the others then knelt down and lifting the little dog from Feea's lap, gently placed it down beside him. Feea reached out and put his hand on Scruff's head; "Bad mans they hurt Scruff an him no wakey up noo. Him no wakey." He started to sob. Jean took him in her arms; "Hush ma wee lamb, hush," she said softly as she tried to comfort him. Feea's mind raced back to a dingy little room where he had heard those words before, and remembered. He looked up into Jean's sad eyes and smiled; "Mammy…" he whispered then slumped forward in her arms, she felt his body go limp as she held him close. Jamie and Curdie arrived and looked down at Jean as she rocked Feea in her arms. When they saw the tears streaming down her face, they knew that Feea was dead. The street singer held Curdie close to his side as the little boy started to cry. Jamie felt a dull pain in his heart as he looked on the heart-rending scene. A light breeze rustled the leaves and somewhere in the old town, Blind Alick was playing 'Ae Fond Kiss' like a lament; it was as if, somehow he knew and was saying goodbye to his little friend.

Darkness was falling when Wullie and Jock decided to check near the bridge again. They started searching in the bushes along the bank of the river. It was high tide and the water was turbulent with strong currents swirling around the old bridge, causing its ancient timbers to creak and groan. The policemen searched until it was getting too dark to see. They sat on one of the low walls at the side of the bridge. The wooden parapets ran from the bridge and curved into the low walls on either side of the road. The two men were thinking about their next move when, in the distance, they could just make out two figures approaching from the town. The outline of their stature showed that one was tall and heavily built and the other quite small and slim. The smaller of the two shuffled rather than walked; this gave them away.

"It's them," Wullie said as he got to his feet, "hide behind this wa' and a'll hide behind the ither yin." The policemen hid behind the walls on either side of the road as the two figures approached. As soon as they stepped onto the bridge, the two policemen appeared from behind the walls. Jock spoke in a loud authoritative voice;

"Monachan and Borland! We'd like a word wae ye!"

The two men looked startled as they turned to face the policemen who had drawn their cudgels. The two officers looked very menacing as they stood with feet apart and holding their cudgels with both hands like a bar, across the lower part of their bodies.

"Whit...Whit dae ye wan't?" The Weasel stammered as Malky looked around for a means of escape, there was only one; and that was across the bridge.

"We're lookin' fur the wee lad called Feea." Wullie said while keeping a close eye on the two men.

"So whit ur ye askin'us fur?" The Weasel replied, cheekily. Wullie's anger was nearing boiling point as he looked the Weasel in the eye; "We know thit ye attacked him and we want tae know where he is. Ah think ye better come alang wae us" The Weasel, with his evil little mind racing and being the treacherous, selfish character that he was, turned on his companion; "It wis him, he telt me thit he stuck the wee boye. It wis him awe richt, ah wisnae even ther." Malky was furious at this deceit. He grabbed the Weasel and threw him into the policemen as he tried to make his escape across the bridge. Wullie struggled with the Weasel as Jock went after the big Irishman. The burly policeman soon realized that he wouldn't be able to catch up with Malky. So, being an expert with the cudgel, he took aim and threw it at the absconding villain. It tangled with his legs and sent him tumbling into the wooden rail at the side of the bridge. The old wood gave way and sent him head long into the swirling currents of the river. Jock ran over and looked down but there was no sign of the Irishman, he had disappeared into the murky depths. Jock turned and looked back towards Wullie who was struggling with the Weasel near the middle of the bridge. He saw Wullie trip and strike his head on the parapet. The big policeman looked dazed and was on his knees as the Weasel picked up a large rock that must have fallen off a cart and was about to bring it crashing down onto Wullie's head. Jock, on realizing that he didn't have time to get back and stop the Weasel's murderous intent, acted swiftly and shouted out;

…"HEY WEASEL! AH THINK THIS IS YOURS!"…

The Weasel turned, and in that second, he saw his own knife come flashing through the air; embed itself deep into his chest. He had a look of total surprise on his face as he stumbled back holding the rock above his head. The motion and the weight of the rock sent him tumbling backwards over the parapet, on his way to joining his companion down the murky road to Hell.

Jock rushed over to his partner who was staggering to his feet.

"Are yae awe richt Wullie?" he said, helping to support the big man who had a trickle of blood running down the side of his face.

"Aye am fine Jock, ah jist feel a wee bit dizzy." He looked around; "Where's Monachan an' Borland? Did they get away?"

Jock had a wry smile on his face as he answered;

"They're awa tae dae a bit o' explainin' tae thur Maker." Wullie looked puzzled; "Dae yae mean…" Jock interrupted his partner; "Aye the Clyde took them alang wae the rest o' the sewage; an' guid riddance."

When the policemen made their way into the Green they were met by the others; Jamie was carrying Feea's body.

"Och dinnae tell me," Wullie said, slowly shaking his head. The look on Jamie's face and the sobbing of Jean and Curdie said it all. No more would they see the little lad dance on the streets of Glasgow.

Jock sighed and went over to Jamie,

"Where did you find him," he said looking at Feea's lifeless body.

"Jean found him in the bushes near the Monument. He died in her erms an' his wee dug's deed as weel. We left it there 'til we could decide whit tae dae. Have you ony idea where we kin fun' the wans thit did this?"

"A widnae' worry aboot them, there weel oan the road tae Hell", Wullie said and spat on the ground. "Aye an' it's by the wei o' the Clyde." Jock added wryly. Jamie understood what he meant and nodded, wishing that he could have been the one who put them there. The small, sad group turned and made their way back into the park.

## A FOND FAREWELL

It was one o' clock in the morning on a clear moonlit night. It was perfectly calm without as much as a breeze to disturb the solemnity of the occasion. The moon shone down on the Monument, giving it an eerie glow.

The small group made their way into Glasgow Green. It was mid-April and the Green was a profusion of golden daffodils. Jamie led carrying Feea's body closely followed by Curdie carrying Scruff. The rest of the group who followed on, consisted of the Reverend Lochart, Wullie and Jock, Blind Alick, Maggie the flower seller, who was carrying a large bunch of roses, Andy McGurk, who owned the stable where Feea slept on occasions and where he was attacked, then there was Mary Anderson, Jean Muldoon, and a group of beggars who knew him well. They made their solemn way to the secret grave that had been dug by Paddy Muldoon, the innkeeper, and Archie Ross, the gravedigger from the churchyard. They had selected a spot near the Nelson Monument, where Feea had performed his greatest feat. It was a fitting location for the little lad and only this small group would know his last resting place. They were all sworn to secrecy; as it was illegal to have a burial on the Green.

When they arrived at the graveside, they found that the other street singers, who travelled with Jamie, had joined Paddy and Archie.

The bottom of the grave had been covered with daffodils and a pillow had been made with primroses.

Jock held Feea while Jamie climbed into the grave, then the burly policeman gently handed the little boy down to the street singer who laid him down. Curdie handed Scruff to Jamie who put him by Feea's side and put the little boy's arm round him; they lay as if they were sleeping together; the way they had always done. With a heavy heart, Jamie stroked Feea's hair then gently put his hand on his head; "Goodbye my little friend," he whispered, then, with a tear running down his face, he climbed out and joined the others. The old minister stepped forward and before beginning his short burial sermon, looked down at Feea lying with his little dog and with a sad smile, remembered the little boy's poignant words; "Dugs keep ye wa'rm aw richt."

"Poor child," he thought to himself, "you'll be warm in the arms of The Lord now; God bless you Feea."

With Paddy Muldoon holding a lantern by his side, he opened his bible and began.

Every one standing there had a memory of Feea.

Andy McGurk recalled that bitterly cold morning when he first met Feea and how his heart went out to him when he saw him lying curled up under the straw with his little dog cowering across him. As he looked down into the grave, he felt a lump in his throat.

The scene was so reminiscent of that New Year's morning. He swallowed hard and slowly shook his head as he bit his lip.

Maggie the flower seller had a tear in her eye as she remembered the day that Feea came to the rescue of a young lady at Glasgow Cross and was gone before she had a chance to thank him. Blind Alick thought back to the night that Feea saved him from the clutches of Malky and the Weasel, a night that he would never forget.

Curdie stood at Jamie's side, and with tears rolling down his face, looked down at his friend, lying there with his little dog, knowing that this was the last time that he would ever see them.

When the minister had finished, a tall figure came out of the shadows.

He silently made his way through the group, and, taking his hat off, knelt beside the grave with his head in his hand." Hushed voices were heard to say; "Look, it's William Caldwell. What is he doing here?" Then they fell silent.

William Caldwell had travelled to Glasgow in an effort to find Feea and take him back to Craigavon, where everyone was waiting to apologise and make up for the injustice that had been meted out to the little lad. Ewan Caldwell had boasted to his friends once too often about how he had turned everyone on the estate against Feea. On that occasion he had been overheard by a friend of his uncle William, who dutifully reported it to him. William's intentions were to adopt Feea and in so doing make him part of a real family.

So it was with a heavy heart that he knelt beside the grave and with a tear running down his face, he whispered a prayer.

"Good bye my little friend, please forgive us," he whispered then he stood up and taking his silk lined cloak off, climbed down into the shallow grave and placed it over Feea and Scruff; then, as silently as he had arrived, he climbed out of the grave and left.

Maggie handed every one a flower; she gave Curdie a rose and told him to drop it in the grave.

The small group watched in silence as Curdie walked over and after a pause, dropped it near Feea's head. The others followed, dropping their individual flowers into the grave then; they gathered handfuls of daffodils and covered the two bodies. Slowly Curdie looked up from the grave and fixed his gaze on the monument. He remembered the numerous times that Feea had tried to show him how to throw a stone over the top and how he could never make it, yet Feea was successful every time. Curdie could still hear his voice; "Say tae yer sel', "me kin dae it", an' ye'll dae it." He bent down and picked up a stone from the pile of earth that had been dug out of the grave.

"A, kin dae it fur you Feea; watch me," he whispered, then with tears streaming down his face, he ran towards the monument while the others looked on, wondering what he was doing. As he approached the monolith, he took aim and threw the stone as hard as he could and without stopping, ran to the other side and looked up to see it appear over the top. He positioned himself to catch it as it came falling towards the ground. Thrusting his right hand up, he caught it and held it tight; but there was something strange, the stone felt different, it felt warm. He opened his hand and instead of the stone that he had picked up, it was Feea's stone; his 'lucky chuckie'. All the sadness and pain welled up inside him and he cried out, "FEEA!...FEEA!"

The echo of his voice faded into the stillness of the night.

**EPILOGUE**

The mist in the Clyde valley grew thicker as Old Hamish Maccurdie whispered the name that he had called out that night at the Nelson Monument.

He clutched the stone to his heart as he felt a sharp pain in his chest. Then, he gasped and fell back on the bench. As his last breath left his body, his hand opened, causing the stone to fall on the ground and role downhill.

Just as it was about to roll into the mist, a foot stopped it. It was a child's foot and it was bare and dirty. A dirty hand reached down and picked up the stone.

"Me wis lookin' fur that," said a familiar voice.

"Whit ur ye sittin' ther fur? Come oan, me is gonnae loup the burn."

With a tear in his eye and a broad grin, young Curdie got up from the bench and ran with Feea into the mist with Scruff yelping at their heels.

The singing of Killiecrankie grew louder as they disappeared back into the past.

# THE END